Steven Camden is one of the UK's most acclaimed spoken-word artists. He writes for stage, radio and screen and teaches storytelling. His creative company Bearheart leads story-based projects across different platforms. Steven moved to London for a girl, but Birmingham is where he's from. He also has a thing for polar bears.

Follow Steven on Twitter:
@homeofpolar

Keep up to date with all Steven's news at:
www.facebook.com/StevenCamdenTheAuthor

Hear from the author himself – Steven Camden's spoken-word poetry can be discovered here:
bit.ly/itsaboutlove

Books by Steven Camden

IT'S ABOUT LOVE

NOBODY REAL

TAPE

NOBODY REAL

STEVEN CAMDEN

HarperCollins *Children's Books*

First published in Great Britain by
HarperCollins *Children's Books* in 2018
First published in the United States of America in this edition by
HarperCollins *Children's Books* 2018
HarperCollins *Children's Books* is a division of HarperCollins*Publishers* Ltd,
HarperCollins Publishers
1 London Bridge Street
London SE1 9GF

The HarperCollins website address is:
www.harpercollins.co.uk
18 19 20 21 22 LSCC 10 9 8 7 6 5 4 3 2 1

ISBN 978–0–00–820679–6

Typeset by Palimpsest Book Production Ltd, Falkirk, Stirlingshire
Printed and bound in the United States of America by LSC Communications

For Lenny,
your music sparked a fire in me
and I am forever grateful.
I love you, man x

PROLOGUE

You're almost twelve.

Staring through the fire at Sean. The tips of the flames lick the top branches of the bush you've both spent all day hollowing out.

You're holding the stolen aerosol can. Sean's nervous smile.

Your willing apprentice.

He can't see me, even though I'm standing right next to him.

You look at the can. Then at me. The flames dance in between us.

"*Do it*," I say.

You smile at Sean, then throw it in.

WEDNESDAY

(14 DAYS LEFT)

THOR BAKER:
FADE COUNSELLING SESSION 1

6PM

I'm sensing resistance.

You are? That's weird.

You don't think this is useful?

I'm sure it's amazing.

That tone is what I'm talking about.

You don't like my tone?

It's not about what I like, Thor. This is about you. Your anger.

Who's angry?

Shall we start?

I thought we had.

Why don't you begin by telling me how you're feeling, right now?

Right now? I'm feeling tired.

OK, and why is that?

I dunno, maybe it's something to do with the fact that I've spent the last week and a half working ten-hour days, demolishing a castle, by myself, my second this month, and tomorrow I'll get a new job and it all starts again. Now, on top of that, I have to come here. For this.

I could move your slot to the mornings if that's better for you?

Whatever you say, Adam.

Alan. You understand the importance of these sessions though, don't you?

How old are you?

Is that important?

You seem young.

You're deflecting now, Thor.

Am I?

Have you been in any fights lately?

Is that in the file?

Yes.

I don't do that any more. I'm done with that. Haven't fought for weeks. Months.

That's good. So knocking down empty buildings is enough to keep your hands busy these days?

Do these look like hands to you?

I'm sorry, paws.

Look, Adam . . .

My name is Alan.

Whatever. I get it. This is your job, to "counsel". That's great, and yes, I've had issues with my temper in the past, but I'm done with that. I've accepted what happened. I've moved on.

I'm glad to hear that, Thor, but this is still compulsory. You have two weeks until the fade. Those of us who were sent away by our makers have a different set of feelings to deal with to those who were simply forgotten.

So you were sent away too?

We're here to talk about you. Can we do that?

There's nothing to say. Ten years ago, she made me. Six years ago, she sent me away; now, in two weeks, none of it matters anyway. I reach ten years, pass through the fade and then that's that. I either grow old and bitter or lose my mind like the zoomers in the park.

And those are the only two options?

What do I know?

That's where I can help.

Who says I need help?

Everyone needs help when they reach the fade. Especially those who were sent away. Unresolved feelings will fester, trust me. If we can talk, I'm sure I can help you transition through it smoothly into the rest of your time.

Just like that.

Thor, I'm not trying to trick you. I understand the feelings. Our makers need us, then they don't need us, and that can leave us lost, but, at the end of the day, we still live on.

They don't know what they need.

OK, a thought, that's good. Would you care to elaborate?

Not really.

Your maker is a girl, right? Marcie? Loves drawing.

Loved.

Right. It says she made you when she was seven, after her mother left?

Nearly eight.

OK, so quite late, and that would make her nearly eighteen now?

I guess so.

Good. See? We're off and running.

Whoopee.

So, by my maths, that would mean she was nearly twelve when she sent you away? Why don't we start with that?

It's all written in your file, isn't it?

Yes, but the point is talking about it. In your words. Can you tell me what happened that last time you were with her?

No.

Because you still feel guilty?

No.

Because you're still angry with her?

No.

Then why?

Because she's an idiot.

☆

Nineteen lights up above the doors.

The screech as the brake squeezes the lift cable and the weight in my stomach rises up into my chest. Doors open. The fur of my arms is flecked with purple plaster dust. The ashes of a castle. Press the warm bucket of chicken against my side and step off into the corridor.

My shadow wipes away as the doors close behind me.

This place is so grey.

Charcoal-coloured doors line the pale, empty walls on both sides, stretching away to the end of the hall where it splits left and right to more walls and more doors.

Some people get to live in castles.

I got a tower block.

As I reach mine, I see a black bin bag slumped against the wall outside next door. Dark and lifeless. Their door's ajar. Must be someone new moving in.

Don't care. Never spoke to whoever left anyway. Not interested.

Just want to eat my chicken and sleep.

✶

Boots off. Close door. Lamp on.

Grab my laptop and slump in my old armchair.

I pop the lid on my chicken and take a deep breath of hot fried comfort. Rocco's chicken is the greatest. I bite into a thick drumstick as I log into the work database.

Glance at the phone on the floor. Think of Blue. Could call her. Should.

Across the room, on the table under the window, the old typewriter sits, waiting.

Ignore it.

I sign off on the castle and request a new job. Got to stay busy. Log out.

Everyone needs help when they reach the fade. Especially those who were sent away.

Alan. What a dick.

Feel the strings of guilt twang in my chest.

Because you're still angry with her?

Drop the bone in the bucket and stare across at the table.

The typewriter. Waiting.

Do these look like hands to you?

Walk to the window.

Dark tower-block tops and the skeleton of a Ferris wheel against a purple-black sky.

Way below on the fuzzy, lit streets, night workers and troublemakers go about their business. Another night in Fridge City.

Sit.

The old black box file of pages. How many are in there now? Enough for a book?

One for every time that I've watched.

Stare at the typewriter. Each letter pitted with dents from my claws.

You wouldn't believe it. Me. Writing.

I close my eyes as I slowly stab at the keys, like every time.

Close my eyes.

To see.

☆

You're on your bed. Legs crossed. Pyjama bottoms and hoodie. Hair up in the high bun you only wear at home. On the duvet next to you, your worn copy of *Othello*, scattered revision cue cards and your old sketchbook.

Your bedside lamp sends a bat-signal beam up at your packed bookshelves. Shelves of ordered comics and graphic novels. Heroes and villains. The lost and the lonely.

You slide the lid of your pen across your bottom lip like lipstick. Thinking.

Tomorrow is your last exam. And you are nervous.

You know what you want to do. But will you be able to do it?

The front door closes downstairs and you hear keys drop on to the phone table. Coral calls up. She has food.

You call down and stare at your sketchbook.

I could help.

I could be there. Nod at the right time. Let you know it's OK.

If you'd just want me.

I'm right here.

So close.

In two weeks, I won't even have this.

Nearly ten years, Marcie.

Do you even know?

THURSDAY

(13 DAYS LEFT)

Wake up like I hit the floor in a dream about falling.

Breathe.

Sunlight strokes my bedroom wall. Warm glow on deep scratches.

City sounds down on the street and the muffled chatter of a morning talk show from next door.

I close my eyes and lie still. Let the morning sink into me.

Hit my punchbag until my shoulders burn. The hiss of air with every connect. The chain link dancing in its bracket.

Shower. Turn the dial until the hot water stings

my neck as I scratch the grout between the tiles with my claw.

Punisher T-shirt and my old jeans. Log into work and print out new job. Coffee. Thick and black.

Feel it hitting my veins as I stare out at the city. Glass buildings twinkle. A sleepy dragon takes off, yawning.

Another day in the not real.

Touch the typewriter. Say your name.

Grab the job printout. And gone.

We look like a handful of X-Men rejects.

A carriage full of forgotten friends heading to the jobs that nobody else wants.

The skinny ghost guy who works by the docks. The bubblegum waitress with the four chunky arms. Moose boy. The old trench-coated hunchback who's always opposite me, muttering to himself. I know everyone's face and nobody's name. The unspoken agreement is: we don't need to speak. We just sit, avoiding eyes, as the high number six train snakes out of the city between impossible skyscrapers, grounded space rockets and hundred-storey tree houses. Jungle-covered pirate ships and giant sleeping dogs. Chocolate factories and looping water slides. Hover cars whizz past us. A flying lion pulls a sparkling carriage. The city circus in full swing.

Another day. Another forgotten structure to destroy.

I feel the same crackle in my gut that I always get on a new job. A fresh building to break down to rubble. Crunch some kid's discarded dreams into dust. Good at it too. Nobody destroys unwanted things better than Thor Baker.

Check my printout. Address is just on the other side of Needle Park. Four stops. Could've walked.

Close my eyes.

Alan. *Everyone needs help. It's good to talk.*

Ball my paws into fists. Yeah. It's good to talk.

But it's so much better to smash.

The street is narrow.

Terraced houses with small, square front yards and shallow bay windows. One of those normal streets in among the madness. This won't take more than a few days.

I don't see anyone, but I can hear Billie Holiday through an open window and there's the warm, soapy smell of fresh laundry. Printout says number seven. Odd numbers are this side.

It's a bit like your street. Coral's street. Different name, but familiar. Where are you now?

Have you already left for school? Outside the gym with everyone else? People swapping last-minute quotes and pretending they haven't revised? You standing silent, telling yourself it's time?

There's a little inky black cat on the low wall outside number nineteen. It looks at me with a tilted head, trying to work out if I'm a threat. A boy with bear arms, carrying a backpack.

I step forward, reaching out to stroke it, but it jumps down and scampers away behind two grey bins.

"Screw you then, kitty."

The cat pokes its head out and stares. I stare back.

"Didn't really want to stroke you anyway, fleabag. Might eat you later."

Carry on walking. Can't wait to start smashing now. Seventeen. Fifteen. Thirteen. Check my bag. The chipped sky-blue of my trusty helmet. If I properly go for it this morning, might even take the afternoon off. Go to the river or something. Eleven. Nine. Yeah. That's a plan. Stop.

Look at the house.

And feel a wrecking ball hit my chest.

☆

The clock ticks.

Ten minutes in

and my page is still empty.

All around me, a gym full of people, sitting in rows, heads bobbing like a gridded flock of feeding birds, speed-scrawling answers to questions we've spent months preparing for.

Every few breaths, a head will pop up, like it heard something. The distant call of that great idea. That one quote that could turn forty UCAS points into forty-eight.

This is it.

Final exam. Sixth form's last supper.

Scan the room. Mouth everyone's name.

Most of us have been at this school since we were eleven. Some of us even went to the same primary school. How many memories do we share?

Izzy Maynard. Tolu Clarke. How different are mine to yours? Eli Hanson. Hardeep Khan. How does it work?

So many versions of everything that happens. Everything that happened.

I remember play fights; you remember getting punched. You remember lunchtimes packed with hide-and-seek; I remember hiding in the craft cupboard and people forgetting about me.

We all remember laughing when Simon Harris tripped and threw pink custard over dicky Mr Page.

When you think about it, it's thirteen years. More than two-thirds of our lives so far sharing the same space and, after today, most of us probably won't see each other again.

We'll say we will, but we won't.

Maybe accidentally in town, one random summer Saturday.

Or five years from now, on a train platform at New Street, heading in different directions.

Or maybe in middle age, at some badly soundtracked class reunion when we're all swollen or wrinkled or both and crying into our gin and tonics about how we chose the wrong path. Isn't that just a little bit weird? Has anyone else in here even thought about it?

Sean is four across and two in front. I watch him

scribble, then pause, scribble then pause. Scratching his head. Questioning himself, whether he's following the right thought.

Cara is two across and three in front. Even from behind, the calm in her slender shoulders is clear.

Prepared. Sure. Tattooing her future on to paper. Ready for the rest of her life. When she's finished, she'll look back, checking in with me. That things are going to plan.

I look down at my page.

Still empty. Still waiting.

I know what I'm supposed to do. And I know what I want to do.

Last chance.

My pen tip scratches the blank paper. Like a claw.

And then I feel you.

For the first time in years. Watching me. Knowing my thoughts.

I look up.

Across the room.

And there you are.

☆

Outside.

The tinted glass facade of reception.

Me, reflected, sitting on the low brick wall, backlit by a fuzzy white afternoon sun.

A life-size, full-page panel. Top left, one thought box.

I did it.

My pen is still in my hand. I actually did it. Can't be undone now.

No more school.

No more lessons.

No more sawdust-dry assemblies.

No more cafeteria parade.

Nearly seven years spent shuffling around this place, nodding at teachers, passing notes, hanging back in cross-country, swapping homework. Come September, somebody else will sit where I sat. Use my locker. Answer the questions I would've answered . . . And a new crop of wide-eyed Year Sevens will step on to the secondary conveyer belt, just as we step off. Into our futures.

My skin is tingling, my whole body buzzing like a light bulb.

And there you are. Behind me. Your reflected silhouette.

Bigger than I remember. Broader. Just me and you in the frame. "I did it, Thor."

Your name is honey in my mouth.

The sliding glass doors of reception part and you're gone.

Cara skips out, arm in arm with Leia and Naomi, like a half-Chinese Dorothy and her friends, off to Oz. A stream of other sixth-formers follows them, squinting as the sunlight hits them. I stand up, and wait for her to see me.

"What the hell, Mars!" she shouts, breaking off from the others and walking over. "How do you do it?"

We're the same height, but my dandelion Afro gives me a few extra centimetres. Cara lifts her arms in celebration and a strip of smooth, pale midriff shows itself above the edge of her skirt.

"How'd you finish so quick?"

I pull my blouse away from my stomach and shrug back. "Said what I wanted to say, I guess."

She smiles. She has more teeth than she needs, little white overlapping roots that on anyone else would look weird, but on her look like evidence of intelligent design.

"Marcie Baker, super-brain," she says, and we hug. I close my eyes and breathe her in.

Honesty, confidence and ambition. That's Cara. Since forever.

"We did it, Mars," she says over my shoulder and squeezes me with her thin arms. I can feel her little pointy boobs pressed against my fuller chest.

"Yeah."

People are scattered down the wide school driveway, hugging and hi-fiving each other. Sean, Mo and Jordan are tearing pages of revision notes into confetti over the bonnets of teachers' cars. Jordan already has his tie around his head. Cara lets go of me and wipes her eyes.

"I feel like I can breathe again, you know?" Her sharp bob shines like black ribbon. "I can't wait for uni! We're gonna have so much fun! Did you do the 'role of women' question?"

I look down at our feet. Her crisp white Vans. My battered Chuck Taylors.

"Yep."

Then she screams. Like a proper animal-type scream, head thrown back, arms stretched out. Someone else behind us takes their cue and screams, then someone else, and someone else, like car alarms triggered by each other, until I'm watching a school driveway full of A-level English students howling at the sky like wolves.

The pack starts to move towards the main gates.

"Everyone's going to Jordan's," says Cara.

"Cool," I say.

She flashes a knowing smile. "You're coming, Mars. Don't you dare even start."

I nod. "OK."

"We did it, Mars! It's done!"

Nod again. It's done.

No undoing it now.

What looks like half our year is sprawled across Jordan's big back garden, like a sixth-form Where's Wally? Shirts are undone. Cigarettes rolled. Detention memories and impressions of teachers are shared. Miss Langley's cleavage. Mr Kelsey's breath. Stormzy's "Shut Up" pumps out through open French doors.

Some people managed to get boxes of wine and cans of Red Stripe from the outdoor, Old Mr Thomas serving teens in school uniform as a "fuck you" to the new Tesco Express.

I sit in the shade of the big oak tree, on a cast-iron garden chair, making cloud prints on the stretched cotton of my navy skirt with the wet bottom of my glass.

I can't tell whether I feel light or heavy. Have I let something go or picked something up?

I scan the party, looking for you. Like you might actually be here. Stupid.

Cara's on the grass, part of a captive horseshoe audience listening to Sean tell a story. His untucked shirt hangs open off his bony shoulders. His limbs have got longer this year.

"You remember, Mars? How mad they were?" he says, looking over, smiling. Audience heads turn my way. I wasn't listening to the story at all.

"Yeah," I say, "course."

Sean waits a second for me to say more, then just dives right back into the narrative, taking his audience with him.

Nabil and David are trying to scale the concrete garage at the bottom of the garden, their shirts long discarded, shoulders gleaming with a sheen of sweat.

I scoop up my stuff just as Nabil gets to his feet on the garage roof like he conquered a mountain.

"I'm gonna jump!" he says. "Somebody film me!"

As people turn to watch, I walk inside.

Jordan's mum's downstairs bathroom is easily the most glamorous bathroom I've ever been in.

From the waist up, the entire wall in front of me is mirror, the sink a chunky white porcelain square set into the glass. The shower cubicle to my right is as big as our entire bathroom, the white towels neatly stacked in a pyramid on the shelves to my left look like they've never been used, and it smells like a swimming pool.

I drop my stuff and stare at myself. My uneven 'fro is wilting. My school blouse grips my chest like my skirt grips my hips. "Full bodied", that's what Coral said, the day she took me for my first proper bra fitting. Standing in the Selfridges changing room, arms out like a new prisoner. Remember it felt like I'd gone from nothing to too much, in one summer. Like my body was some fast-tracked puberty experiment. Cara's face when she came back from France. She wanted to be the one who got boobs first.

There's nothing more attractive than a full-bodied woman, Coral said. Just look through history, real history: full-bodied women are nature's queens.

Not really the most humble way to describe yourself in Freshers' Week though, is it? Yeah, hi, I'm Marcie Baker, I'm from Birmingham, I'm into reading and films, I used to draw a bit, oh, and I have the attractive, full body of a natural queen.

Something about this mirror having no edge makes it feel less like looking at my reflection and more like staring at someone else. A nearly eighteen-year-old girl.

I make myself smile and she smiles back. Smooth cheeks, more dark freckles than a face needs. The gap between her two front teeth is big enough to be embarrassing. An unwanted hereditary gift from a woman long gone.

I close my eyes. And breathe.

"You look older."

My body stiffens.

You're standing behind me, big enough to almost completely block the door.

I can hear muffled laughter from outside.

You step forward. The light hits your cheekbones. Your hero's jawline. Is there a trace of stubble?

"So do you," I say, keeping a straight face, trying to ignore the fact that I can feel my heart beat in my skin.

"I guess we both do," you say. A shrug of your bear shoulders.

My fingers grip the seams of my skirt. "What are you doing here, Thor?"

"I don't know. You tell me."

I swallow and watch your eyes scan my reflection up and down.

"You can't be here."

Your eyes meet mine. "Says who?"

Then we just breathe and stare at each other. How long has it been?

"I did it, Thor."

Your wicked smile.

"I saw."

"Mars?" Cara bangs on the door and you disappear.

"Mars? You OK?"

"Yeah, I'm fine. Just washing my hands!"

I push the lever on the swan-neck tap and swill my face with cold water.

The empty space in the mirror.

"You sure you're OK? You look kinda pale."

Cara's concerned face, her cheeks slightly flushed from cheap wine.

"Yeah, I just feel a bit off. I didn't eat. I think I'm gonna go."

"You want me to come with you? We could get chicken?"

"Nah, I'm good, you stay, have fun."

"You sure?"

"Yeah. Message me later if I miss anything."

Her expression turns sheepish. "Nothing's gonna happen. I've left it too long. He's oblivious," she sighs. "That ship has sailed."

I smile and poke her stomach. "Maybe, but you've always been a strong swimmer."

She hugs me again. "I love you, Marcie Baker."

"I love you too, Cara Miles-Yeung."

Our bodies shake with laughter and I go to squeeze her, just as she pulls away.

The bin men haven't been.

One black bag leans on the wall under the hedge with a trail of its guts on the pavement. A bloated green tea bag, a clump of brown rice, the wilted carcass of a red bell pepper. It's a miniature art installation made by a fox.

I step over the exhibit, through the gate and see the sign. It's one of those cheap banners you buy from a card shop. CONGRATULATIONS! in somebody with zero style's idea of exciting letters. I can hear Stevie Wonder singing inside. Coral always makes an effort.

Think of the end of *Jurassic Park* when the T. rex is roaring as the torn banner ripples down from the ceiling. Close my eyes.

You came, Thor. I needed you there and you came.

Nobody knows. Only us.

Open my eyes. Tear down the banner. And go inside.

☆

Dusk. And I'm literally buzzing.

If you could press mute on these busy city streets and lean in, you'd hear my body crackling like a plasma ball.

I crossed over. To you. You saw me. There. In the real. And I helped.

You know I did.

At the lights, I lean on the stop sign as a fifteen-metre white limousine rolls past. Across the street, a line of five black-suited yakuza sit in the neon window of a noodle bar, slurping in unison, their dark sunglasses hiding their eyes.

The house is the bridge. Coral's house. Has it always been there – just across the park – this whole time?

Walking in. The hall. The stairs. Your bedroom door. The heat in my chest.

A foghorn.

I look up and see a World War II German Royal Tiger tank waiting at the red light. The top hatch creaks open and a small man wearing military uniform and a white moustache as big as a broom head starts barking unintelligible orders.

I cross the street.

Why now? Why do I find the house now?

I stop on the corner. The grinding tread of the tank behind me. The neon of the noodle bar.

The fade.

Ten years since you made me. Six since you sent me away.

I finally have a new way to reach you.

And I have to knock it down.

The bin bag is still there outside next door.

The door is closed and I don't hear anything

from inside. Why wouldn't they just take it to the rubbish chute? I'm not doing it. Not my job.

Inside.

Boots off.

My head is swimming. It happened. I was there. With you. Through the house, that I now have to destroy.

Alan. *Unresolved feeling will fester, Thor.*

No shit.

Who can I tell?

No one. No one can know, Marcie. Just me and you.

The need to see you pulls me to the table. The old typewriter smiles. Like it knows.

Like it knows.

☆

You're drying a dinner plate.

Coral stands next to you, washing the last of the dishes. Her Lauryn Hill *MTV Unplugged* album is playing from the living room. She hums along as she washes.

You thank her for dinner and for the banner and the cake. She tells you not to be silly and offers to drop you off wherever Cara and the others are. You tell her you're tired and that you're just going to watch a film and, as she passes you the pan, you notice a mobile phone number inked on the back of her hand.

You ask her if she realises that it's nearly ten years since you moved in with her. Coral drops the sponge. Of course she remembers it, she says. She remembers it like it was yesterday. She tells you that becoming your legal guardian is the best thing that ever happened to her.

You smile.

She asks if you've seen your dad. You tell her you'll go tomorrow.

She pulls you in for a hug and tells you that she is so proud of you and that you are so smart and so special and that university is going to be the best time of your life and, as she kisses you on the head, you close your eyes and see me.

FRIDAY

(12 DAYS LEFT)

Diane's gift-wrapping a slim hardback for an old man with a crooked spine and long ears.

They're the only two people in the shop.

Street sounds are muffled as I close the door gently behind me. Deep breath.

The calm of being surrounded by books.

Something folky is playing quietly through the wooden speakers behind the till.

"Morning, Marcie," says Diane, in her PhD voice. She's wearing one of her self-knitted cardigans over a sky-blue denim shirt buttoned up to her slender neck. Hipster bookshop chic.

The old man is watching her fingers gracefully wrap the book, like a young boy watching his grandfather fix a precious watch. He gives a grateful nod as Diane hands him the finished gift and then he just stands there, like he doesn't want their interaction to be over.

"Have a lovely day," Diane says to him, and I get a little bit of leftover smile as he leaves.

"Bless him. That's the third time he's been in this week."

"I think he likes you," I say, dropping my jacket over the chair behind the counter.

"He's sweet. I wonder who he's buying them for?"

"Maybe it's no one. Maybe they're for himself, and he just loves opening presents."

Diane looks at me, her glasses resting on top of her Disney-heroine hair.

"That's so sad, Marcie."

"Is it?"

I watch her try to see it my way. Her thinking face makes her look like a little girl. I'm not sure how old she actually is. Old enough to be doing a literary doctorate and to like Nirvana in a non-retro way. Old enough to be having a not-so-covert thing with Dad and it not be creepy. Early thirties? Pretty and clever and slightly vacant in the eyes. She's the most English person I know.

"How is he?" I say, pointing at the ceiling.

Diane pulls a pained expression. "He's 'working'," and the way she rolls her eyes tells me it was a long night.

"I'm just gonna go say hi. Do you want a coffee?"

Diane zones out, like she's contemplating a tough life decision, then snaps back. "I'd love one, please. Wait, are you done? Last exam?"

"Yep. All finished."

"Congratulations! You must feel amazing."

"I guess so."

"You're going to love uni, Mars, trust me."

I nod. She smiles again, then gets on with her stock check. I run my fingers along the spines as I walk, giving my usual wink to Johnny Cash, staring out from his autobiography in the music and film section next to the door for the stairs.

It looks like somebody poured a skip-load of paper through the skylight. A snowdrift of empty white A4 curves up the walls of the small shaded room at the top of the stairs.

There's a kind of path, where someone has waded through the middle. I can hear Dad muttering as I follow it to the open living-room door.

He's in the corner, past the sofa, standing on his head.

"What are you doing, Dad?"

His eyes stay closed, still mumbling something to himself.

"Dad."

He slowly lowers his bare feet and stands, blinking slowly, readjusting to being the right way up.

"Better. Feel my face." He pushes back his black pipe-cleaner hair. I don't move.

"Come on. Feel my face."

He takes my hand and presses it against his cheek. His skin is stubble-rough over sharp cheekbones. "You feel that? Morning, gorgeous."

He leans in and kisses my cheek. I smell Imperial Leather soap and tobacco.

"Circulation, Mars. You know, in some cultures people believe that ideas exist in the blood. More blood to brain, more ideas." He taps his temple.

"So vampires must be geniuses then," I say, looking out of the tall window on to the sleepy high street.

Dad smiles and sits down at the little table. His yellow legal notepad is pristinely empty.

"Exactly." He starts to roll a cigarette. "Is it Saturday already?"

"It's Friday, Dad."

"Don't you have an exam?"

"I finished. Yesterday."

Dad jumps up like someone just tasered his arse. "Yes! Freedom! Come here!"

"I still have to wait for results, Dad."

He lets go. "Who cares about results?"

"Erm, UCAS? The universities?"

"You've aced them. Coral's academic skills have rubbed off."

"I'm glad you're so sure, Dad."

Dad's not listening. "We should celebrate! This is the best summer ever. No more school, getting ready to leave. Have you got any weed?"

"Dad . . ."

"No, course." He nods to himself. "Is that my shirt?"

"No, it's mine."

"Hmm. Looks like one I used to have." He sits back down and finishes rolling his cigarette.

"I'm just here for coffee," I say. "You want one?"

The kitchen is a thin sideboard city of dirty dishes and hanging pans.

There's still half a large glass bowl of tar-black coffee in the diner-style maker.

"How's my big sister?"

I pretend I haven't heard him as I search for the least dirty cups and swill them out.

"Did she get you a gift? I bet she got you a gift."

I bring the pot through and Dad holds up his empty cup.

"What was it, vouchers? Coral loves her vouchers."

"No gift needed, Dad." I pour. He raises a finger.

"I'll get you something then! What do you need? I could get you a new sketchbook?"

"Still got the last one, thanks."

"Anything in it?" he says, his smile almost desperate.

"Not really."

His face drops for a second. "Can't rush ideas, Mars. New trainers then?"

"From the man who doesn't even own a pair of socks?"

He lights his cigarette. "I do own socks! I have multiple pairs of socks. Casual socks, dress socks, sports socks."

"Yeah?"

"Just because a person doesn't reveal something doesn't mean it doesn't exist. Besides, socks are for sheep, Mars. I want to feel what I'm walking on."

"How convenient." I nod towards the small room full of paper. "Busy night?"

Dad blows smoke. "All part of the process, my young padawan. Did Diane seem pissed off to you?"

"Not particularly."

"Excellent." He sips his coffee. "I'm getting closer, Mars, I can feel it." He moves his fingers like he's playing piano in the air.

"That's great, Dad." I go back to the kitchen and pour coffee for me and Diane.

"You sure you don't have any weed? Even a little resin?"

"Dad, please," I say, carrying the mugs into the living room. "How many times? I don't smoke."

"Well, you should. You're nearly eighteen; you'll be at uni soon. Poetry readings and squat parties."

"It's not Greenwich Village in the fifties, Dad."

"Very funny, Mars. I'm just saying, you should be experimenting at your age. Poking out of the box."

"And what box is that, O wise one?"

He takes a long pull on his cigarette. In his white vest and brown trousers, his unruly hair pushed back, he looks part beatnik, part mad scientist. A man who operates just off the pulse, who believes in conspiracy theories and who, some days, completely forgets to eat.

"Well, if you have to ask, it might already be too late."

I exaggerate a sad face. "I guess I'll just go downstairs and get back in my box then."

Dad's face turns serious. "I'm proud of you, special girl. You did it."

I stare at the coffee mugs, feeling your name running down the corridors in my head. Scratching the walls. Banging doors. You did it.

"Don't be too proud yet, Dad. Results aren't till August."

Dad shakes his head and picks a stray tobacco strand from his lip. "Please. Pass. Fail. F. A-star. Just labels, Mars. You're not a can of beans. Life is process."

He smiles the kind of smile that makes it easy to imagine him as a cheeky five-year-old, crayoning the walls with ideas.

"Get back to work," I say, and I walk out of the room.

"I'm getting close, Mars. Really close. I feel it!"

I kick through the blank paper, heading back to the stairs.

Once every ten years, a novel comes along that makes all the rest look at each other and say, "What the hell do we do now?" Baker's daring debut is that book, and, if you are at all interested in where contemporary storytelling is heading, I advise you to read it.

– Quentin Quince, the *Times Literary Review*, on *Dark Corners* by Karl Baker

Karl Baker.

Award-winning debut writer.

Giver of half my genetic code.

Barely capable of looking after himself.

Still working on his second novel seven years later.

"You OK, Marcie?"

Diane's face is wrinkled up like she's trying to read Latin.

"What? I'm fine."

I don't know how long I've been standing here, holding two coffees.

"It's just . . . you looked, well, drunk."

"I was just thinking."

I pass her a mug.

"Thanks. Your phone beeped a couple of times."

Probably Cara. "Thanks."

"Just thinking, eh?"

"Yeah."

"I hear you. So do you think you'll be around more over the summer?"

"I don't know. I guess. Not much else to do."

"Great. That's good."

We both stare out of the front windows either side of the shop door.

Diane sips. "It's nice to hang out, isn't it?"

"Yeah."

Still staring.

"Did he say anything, about me?"

I sip. Hot, bitter coffee on my tongue.

"What do you mean?"

"Nothing. Doesn't matter. I like your shirt. Is it new?"

"No."

"Cool."

The shop is one square room with the till in the centre next to a thick supporting pillar. The layout hasn't changed since Dad bought it nearly three years ago – four small display tables, one in each quarter: new and contemporary fiction; classics and historical stuff; non-fiction; and children and teen.

It used to be called Blue Pelican Books, but Dad sanded the name off the shopfront the day he moved in. He said you can't trust any animal with wings.

There's never been what you'd call a steady stream of customers, especially on weekdays, and, since the new Foyles opened up in town, things on the outskirts have got even quieter. We still get new releases, just fewer copies, and people rarely wait for an order when there's Amazon Prime two clicks away. Luckily, the romance of the underdog hasn't completely died out so things just about tick over. Diane moved into the downstairs back room and basically runs the place, with me helping out on Saturdays and when I'm free. Dad pays me bits here and there, but I do it mostly for the peace. I can read, scribble stuff down if the mood takes me, or just do nothing. No questions or hassles. No Facebook updates or plans for the future. A haven.

My haven.

"I might go get a sandwich. Do you want a sandwich, Diane?"

"Yes, sandwich. Definitely."

"Great." I put down my coffee. "Crisps?"

"Are you having crisps?"

"Probably."

"Ooh, can we have Monster Munch?"

I don't even think she realises she's speaking to me like I'm four. Some people can't gauge tone at all. I nod excitedly. "Yeah! Let's!"

A stab of guilt from my own sarcasm. Then Diane claps, like actually claps, and for some reason so do I.

We're both clapping, like sugar-charged babies, about crisps.

It's funny how much of life can feel like a Year Ten drama exercise.

Drake and Rihanna singing about work.

I lay my basket on the self-checkout shelf.

Things are changing.

Scan an item to start.

Tuna and sweetcorn on wholemeal bread. Beep.

English Language and Literature, Psychology and Biology A levels. Beep.

Pickled onion Monster Munch. Beep.

Three grade As needed for entry to Psychology undergraduate degree. Beep.

The old woman at the next till along can't find the barcode on her slab of cheddar.

Chicken, bacon and avocado roll. Beep.

Leaving home. Beep. Following Cara.

A skinny man with arm tattoos and a supermarket polo shirt comes to help her.

Flamin' Hot Monster Munch. Beep.

New city. Beep.

A mountain of student loans. Beep.

Bottle of still water. Beep.

Three more years of study. Beep.

The foundation for a life. Beep. For what?

Can of Coke.

For who?

Can of Coke.

Hold it. Look at the rest of the stuff in my 5p carrier bag. Shop noise and an auto-tuned pop chorus. Work, work, work, work, work, work.

Can of Coke.

Rest of my life.

Can of Coke.

What have I—

"Do it."

You're standing behind me, half your face reflected in the screen.

"Please scan an item, or press finish to pay." The robotic teacher voice of the till.

My heart.

The businessman waiting behind me is head down in his phone.

Stare at the can in my hand. Look at our reflection. Smiling. The crackle in my stomach.

I press finish, resting the can on the edge of the barcode glass as I feed a ten-pound note into the machine. The whir. The guy with the tattoos is helping the old woman with the rest of her stuff. His back is turned. My change falls into the plastic tray like fruit-machine winnings.

I lift the bag off the scales and put the stolen can inside, scoop out my change and walk away, leaving my receipt.

Scattered pensioners, filing in and out of the charity shops.

I can feel you over my right shoulder as I walk. This side of the street has the shade.

Push my phone on to vibrate and hold it to my ear like I'm making a call.

"That was so stupid," I say as I pass Subway and catch a waft of vacuum-packed vomit.

"Felt good though, right?"

I don't look at you. "What do you want, Thor?"

You move closer. "What do you want, shoplifter?"

I swerve to pass a shuffling old man wearing three different shades of pastel blue.

"I'm not a kid any more," I say.

"Neither am I."

You step up so you're level with me. "Tell me that didn't feel good though."

I stop walking.

"It didn't feel good."

You shake your head.

"So why are you smiling?"

Then my phone vibrates for real and slips out of my hand. I scramble to catch it, smacking my shopping bag on the pavement and nearly falling over as the phone lands in my palm.

"Nice catch." You stand there, clapping your paws.

Cara's face, beaming out from my phone screen.

I stand up straight and compose myself. "This is a bad idea, Thor."

You nod.

"Probably."

And then you're gone.

The old man tips his sky-blue flat cap as he slowly steps through the space where you were.

I nod back, then answer the call.

"Marcie! It's a full house tonight!"

Cara's dad Ken always greets me like I'm an old schoolfriend he hasn't seen for years.

He's a graphic designer and he looks like one. Bald like he did it on purpose, he's got that flawless, poreless, older man skin that says water filters and gym membership. He's holding an expensive-looking tea towel.

"Full house?"

Ken nods. "Morgan's here. Hungry?"

It smells amazing. Don't think I've ever been to Cara's house and Ken hasn't been cooking. I've had so many foods for the first time here. Wild boar. Quinoa. Pickled herring.

"Her highness is upstairs working on a new video. Dinner in a hour, OK?"

"OK, Ken. Thank you."

And he's off, back towards their massive kitchen, expensive tea towel over his shoulder, leaving me to close the front door, like I'm family.

Cara already has the tripod and camera set up when I knock and walk in. She's checking her camera angles, deliberating over which pillows to have in shot.

"I'm not dressing up, Car."

Cara stops fluffing pillows. "Who said anything about dressing up?"

I throw my jacket over the back of her 1970s super-villain swivel chair.

Cara's room is like a cross between an FBI investigation wall and a retro furniture shop. The walls are collages of magazine articles, photographs and old B-movie posters. I always think of people's bedrooms being like the inside of their head. Cara's is busy and full, but organised. She was made for her journalism degree. Her hair's tied up in a stubby ponytail and she's wearing her pre-planned "I just threw anything on" outfit for the camera: black leggings and one of Morgan's old sweaters.

"Morgan's home?"

"Apparently," she says.

"That's early, no?"

"Dunno. Haven't seen him. Been in his room since he got back. If he's home early, he must be broke."

"I haven't seen him for ages," I say.

Cara cuts me a disapproving look on her way to her backstage-style dresser.

"Don't worry, you can stare longingly into his eyes over dinner. That's if he even comes down."

"Shut up."

I try to think of the last time I saw Morgan. Maybe the Christmas before last. He rarely comes home from university in London.

"Can't we just hang out, Car?"

"We are hanging out."

"Yeah, but I mean just do nothing. Exams are over. When was the last time we just did nothing?"

Cara looks at me like I'm speaking Swahili.

Through her bedroom window, the sky is going dark. I picture the view from across the street. Camera on tripod, one girl fluffing pillows, getting ready, another standing nervously next to the bed. Some girls make thousands of pounds on their own in their rooms with their laptops.

"What accents can you do?" she says, pulling two bottles of what look like shampoo out of a yellow Selfridges bag, one seaweed green, one milk-chocolate brown.

"Accents? What are you talking about? What are they?"

Her face lights up.

"I had an idea."

What started as a simple Year Ten drama project quite quickly evolved into Cara's performance-art YouTube channel Jumblemind.

Jumblemind is basically a space where all of Cara's social-commentary ideas are sporadically filmed and uploaded to an audience of 316 subscribers made up mostly of younger girls from school. Any little nugget of performance gold that's been rattling around her head gets dumped out on film for her cult following's consumption and, over the years, a high percentage of these nuggets have involved yours truly.

October 3rd 2014: "Genderrorists" – The two of us stand back to back, reading extracts from *The Vagina Monologues* in balaclavas.

February 9th 2015: "Pressure to Make Up" – Cara uses the latest, top-of-the-range L'Oréal products to paint my face to look like Heath Ledger's Joker.

My personal favourite though was this time last year, when Cara just sat in front of the camera for ten minutes, stuffing an entire Black Forest gateau into her mouth and crying.

OMG! Don't know why but can't stop watching! So dumb but SOOO good! LOL!!!

– YouTube comment on "Gateau Tragic" from Trixabell496

"You'll need to put your hair up," she says. "There's bobbles in the bedside drawer."

"Car, what are we doing?"

"It's a goodbye to school." She holds up the bottles like she just won them in a raffle.

"Face-pack Shakespeare!"

The car still smells like new trainers.

Cara's humming along to Lana Del Rey, effortlessly driving down dark streets towards mine, like she's had her own taxi for twenty years.

It's probably testament to her charm that getting a brand-new black Mini Cooper for her eighteenth birthday didn't make me want to punch her in the face. I had the grand total of three empty supermarket driving lessons with Coral before we both decided I might be more suited to the passenger seat, for now.

"I can hear you thinking, you know," she says.

"Imagine."

"He's such a dick."

"Who is?"

"My brother. Can't even come down to dinner? Locking himself away in his room? You know, I probably won't even see him before he goes back. He hasn't asked about the exams once. Nothing."

"Maybe he's busy."

"Oh, shut up. Stop defending your prince."

Her arm goes up to protect herself as she laughs. I just give her the finger.

"We could drive up to Leeds?" she says. "For the day, start getting to know our new home before September." Excitement radiates off her as she speaks. It's hard not to be drawn to someone who's completely sure of what they want. "I could maybe even get Dad to sort a hotel. He gets things on account sometimes." She pulls into the petrol station forecourt and parks next to the pump. The stereo display goes black as she turns off the engine, then flickers back to life.

High halogen floodlights turn up the contrast of the colours through the glass of the kiosk and make me think of that Edward Hopper painting, *Nighthawks*.

"Mars? Are you listening?"

"Did you ever have an imaginary friend?" I ask.

"An imaginary friend?"

"Yeah."

"Like when I was a kid?"

"Yeah."

"No. Why?"

"No reason."

"You did, blatantly, right?"

I shrug.

"Course you did," she says.

"What does that mean?"

"It means I can see it: you in the park, talking to an empty swing."

"Thanks a lot, Car."

"No, it's a compliment. I wanted one. Some super-badass flying ninja princess goddess. I just never did it. Too busy writing pretend newspaper reports on my family.

I would've been so jealous if I'd known you back then. An imaginary friend would've been amazing!"

"You think?"

"Yeah! Someone who gets you? Who you don't have to pretend with? What was her name, your one?"

I squeeze my thumb in my lap.

"I don't remember."

Cara takes her purse from the tray under the stereo.

"No matter, you've got me now, eh?"

She smiles, then gets out.

I lean over so I can see into the rear-view mirror. The empty back seat.

Where are you right now, Thor Baker?

☆

How many times have I stood in this lift?

Stared up at these numbers?

Ten years. A decade. Decayed.

Think of my first day. The day you made me. Crossing over after you fell asleep. Waiting in line. Filling out forms like everyone else. The grand City Hall full of fresh immigrants to the

not real. Standing in our rows, staring forward, hands raised, reciting the oath.

Less than two weeks to go, Marcie.

What do I do?

The fade is coming. I can't fight it. Can I?

No.

I have to destroy the house. But, once it's gone, so are you. Forever. A pile of rubble. And I just live out the rest of my days here, like the others.

The lift doors open and I stare down my grey corridor. The fade is coming.

And I don't want to be alone.

The doors start to close again and I let them.

I know who'll understand.

"These blessed candles of the night."

Leyland's voice has the velvet quality of cello notes. When most people quote Shakespeare, it sounds like they're trying to seem clever. When Leyland does it, it's like the words are his own.

Leaning on the ledge of the roof next to him, looking down at the city, it feels like we're on stage for an audience of night sky.

The air is sharp.

I don't come up here as much as I used to. Blue thinks it's weird that I still visit my elder at all, but just the right amount of time with Leyland can feel like the kind of dream you wake up from smiling.

"To what do I owe this pleasure, Mr Baker?" he says.

"Just wanted to see how you were," I lie. "It's been a while."

He looks at me.

"What?"

"You have many skills, my young friend, but sharing untruths is not one of them."

"It's nearly ten years, Leyland."

"Ah. Of course." His eyes widen. "The fade."

I push myself up to standing. I'm a full head taller and almost twice as wide, but when I'm around him I always feel like the nervous apprentice. Leyland turns his back on the city and folds his arms. "And you feel . . . scared?"

"No! I'm not scared. Scared of what?"

He takes a white packet of cigarettes out of his corduroy breast pocket. "Precisely."

Tapping one out like a private detective, he sparks it with his smooth silver lighter. He's got one of those Philip Marlowe faces. Straight lines and deep creases. Thin lips and neck, dark eyes and slick hair. The kind of head that screams out for a fedora. He was my assigned elder when I was first made. Most people lose touch with theirs once they settle, but Leyland and I became friends.

I picture the house. The stairs. Your bedroom door.

"Ten years comes to us all eventually, Thor," he says, turning to face the city again, leaning on the edge. "How long since she sent you away?"

"Six years." I pick at the rough stone with a claw. "I know I should be ready for it. I just feel . . . messy."

Leyland smokes slowly for a while, then says, "To find a form that accommodates the mess, that is the task of the artist."

I must've heard him speak hundreds of these kinds of quotes over the years. Each one somehow managing a perfect blend of just enough possible relevance mixed with a thick, cloudy ambiguity.

"Is this what you felt like when you hit the fade?"

Leyland does one of his dramatic, slow-motion blinks. "I'd have to imagine it was, yes. Long time ago now, of course, and I'm not sure how apt the word 'hit' is. I seem to recall it feeling more like crawling."

A metal aerial creaks behind us as he takes another long drag. "We are different from most others, Thor, you and I. You must remember that. We have to deal with things only those who were sent away can understand. To be simply forgotten is one thing, but to be sent away, to have the door slammed firmly in your face, that . . . that is an entirely different box of snakes."

I lean next to him. Cold air ripples through the hair on my arms.

"The fade takes many forms for those sent away," he says, pointing at me with his cigarette. "Each one of us gets our own test. And it always makes the most tragic of sense."

High above us, wisps of silver cloud drift across the darkness.

"How long will I be angry, Leyland? How long were you angry?"

Leyland closes his eyes. Smoke curls up past his face into the night.

"Oh, I'm still angry, Thor, believe me. I'm still angry enough for the both of us."

The bin bag is still there, propped against the wall.

Why haven't they moved it? Who moved in?

Don't care. Not my problem.

It's past midnight. Didn't tell Leyland about the house. About crossing over. Couldn't face the lecture. I won't tell anyone, Marcie.

You'll be asleep now. I won't watch for long.

Open my door.

"Finally! I was about to leave."

Blue's sitting in my chair sideways, her slim legs dangling over the arm, chunky silver headphones in her lap. I recognise her oversized black hoodie. It's mine. My skull feels like it's shrinking.

"Are you coming in?"

I drop my bag and kick off my boots. Blue swings her legs round to sit properly. Her perfect fringe is like a blonde roof for her pale, princess face.

"You didn't have anything to drink," she says, holding up a brown paper bag.

"I'm fine with the tap," I say, closing the door, my body filling up with guilt.

"Where you been?" she says, looking at me like a prosecution lawyer. I don't blink.

"Helping Leyland."

"How is the Mad Hatter?"

"Don't call him that. What time is it anyway?"

Blue pulls the thin glass bottle out of the bag.

"Time for a drink."

"We should talk, right?" I say, staring into the black mirror of the kitchen window.

Blue's at the counter, pouring something dangerous into coffee mugs.

"That's not why I came, Thor."

She holds out a mug, smiling. She's pretty. Even more so because she tries to hide it. Princess Blue. Denier of powers. Hider of privilege.

I lean against the sink. "Blue, listen, I've been meaning to call. I—"

"Shut up, yeah? Talking doesn't get us anywhere."

She takes a cowboy-style gulp, blinks and smiles again.

I look down into my mug, the dark bronze of trouble. "I don't think it's a good idea."

She finishes her drink and pours herself another one. "What, us hanging out? Just 'friends', remember? Wait, you thought I came here to . . .?" she frowns. "Don't flatter yourself, Thor Baker."

She knocks back her drink in one, then pours another. I put mine down.

"Hang out?" I say. "Don't you have to actually like someone's company to hang out?"

Blue sighs. "Nope. I hang out with idiots all the time." A wicked smile.

"How's work?" I say, and her shoulders slump.

"Same, same," she says. "We do what we can, but we're basically babysitters. We bring supplies to the park, feed them and make sure they're comfortable." She downs her drink and pours again.

"Anyway, enough violins. I've been leading some workshops with newbies."

"Really? You?"

"Don't looked so shocked, Baker. I have to try and balance things out, right? It's just helping them find their feet." She sits down at the little table with her drink. "Man, some of them are so small! Do you remember it, when you first came?"

"Course," I say. "So do the newbies know who you are?"

"I'm Blue. What else do they need to know?"

"Course. Don't want anyone loving you for powers first, right?"

She shakes her head, "Don't want anyone loving me full stop."

Silence.

I first met her at Needle Park. It was just before Christmas, the year I was sent away. She was handing out soup to a crowd by the fountain.

Something about how she moved got me. A slow kind of grace. Like she didn't need to try. Like someone who knows they can fly and chooses not to. In her case, literally. In a circle of people wishing they were more, the person wishing she was less shone like a diamond in a dumpster.

We were never officially "a thing", but stuff happened.

"What about you?" she says. "You start your fade counselling yet?"

I sit down opposite her, familiarity seeping into the room.

"Started Wednesday."

"And?"

"And what? Stupid pop psychology crap. Anger issues from being sent away. It's good to talk. Blah-blah-blah."

"Helpful though, right? I remember it helping."

"Who says I need help?"

Silence.

I tap the table with one claw. "It's not a big deal. I'm gonna hit ten years, like everyone does, and then just . . . carry on. It's not like I'm gonna flip out or something."

Her look says it all.

"That's different," I say. "The ones you work with, they're . . ."

"They're what, Baker? Different? Weak? You think it can't happen to you?"

"Blue, I'm fine. I've moved on. Can we drop it now?"

She finishes her drink and gets up to pour another. "So you've stopped watching?"

I fight my instinct to look away. Blue smiles like an older sister who already knows you've been in her room and touched her stuff. Lie? Truth? Lie? Truth?

"I have actually. Are you planning on drinking the whole bottle?"

Blue turns around with her mug. "So, if I were to walk in there right now and inspect that typewriter, it'd be covered in dust? And, if I broke open that box, I wouldn't find new pages?"

Don't flinch. Don't flinch. "No."

Silence. "Go check if you want." Straight face. Straight face.

She shakes her head.

"Good," I say. "I told you. I'm done with her. She can do what she wants. My life is here."

Blue nods, tentatively. I need more.

"I'm serious, Blue. I'm even knocking down her house, for God's sake."

"What?"

The release of finally telling someone, even for the wrong reasons.

"Her house. They sent me there. New job. I'm demolishing the house she made me in."

The shock on Blue's face melts into disbelief, then happiness, then comes back round to shock again.

"Wow. And you've started already?"

"Yeah. Today."

"And you're OK?"

I stand up. "I'm fine. It's time. I told you, I'm done with her."

And she hugs me, standing on her tiptoes, pulling me down to her level, squeezing me, and I can feel the warmth of her relief. I try to push out my guilt and just enjoy the hug. The moment. It's not until you get a good one that you remember how amazing hugs can be.

Blue slips back down on to her feet, holding my paws in her hands.

“Have you been fighting again?”

“No. It’s from work. I’m done with the fighting too.”

Guilt in my spine.

She looks up at me. “Can I stop over?”

“Blue . . .”

“Just to sleep.”

Smell the booze on her breath. See the hope in her eyes. Smile.

“Course you can.”

We hug again and she speaks into my chest. “I missed you, Thor.”

Squeeze.

“I missed you too, Blue.”

And I have. Truly.

So maybe I’m only half a liar.

SATURDAY

(11 DAYS LEFT)

"Bad dream?"

Blue on her side, smiling at me with sleepy eyes. I realise I'm gripping twisted duvet in my paws and let go. Breathe out. "I'm OK."

She strokes the fur on my shoulder. "Let's go out by the river," she says, covering her mouth with her other hand, worried about morning breath. "We could take some food. Drop rocks into the water, remember?"

I do remember. Her skimming stones. Me shot-putting boulders. But I want you.

"I have to work."

Her hand leaves my fur. "It's Saturday, Thor."

"I know."

"I'm not saying it has to mean anything. Just

two friends hanging out by the river. It'll be fun."

Sit up.

"It's not that, Blue. I have to put in braces on the side walls, so I don't damage the buildings either side."

"But it's the weekend."

"I know. The removals guys have to come first thing Monday and, if the braces aren't in place, we can't do the clearing."

She's scowling.

"I'm serious," I say. "It's not like a castle. It's not all just mindless smashing up, you know. There is some skill involved. I'm not just some animal."

She smiles and touches my shoulder again. "I like you, animal."

I am a liar. Say something true.

"I'll cook later; you could come over?"

"You'll cook?"

"OK, I'll get Rocco's. How long since we had chicken?"

"Too long."

"Exactly. Say, nine?"

She nods. I get out of bed, part of me wishing I could step out of my skin and leave the me she wants there with her.

She deserves more than I really am.

☆

Dad looks like a scarecrow trying to defuse a nuclear bomb.

I think I've seen him behind the till maybe three times since he bought the place.

Customer service isn't his calling.

A woman and her little nursery-age daughter are in the children's corner, looking at picture books. The old crooked man who's in love with Diane is browsing classic fiction.

"Marcie, thank God!" says Dad, holding his head. "This thing hates me."

I step behind the counter. The old monitor screen is showing "system error".

"What did you do, Dad?"

"Me? I didn't do anything. It's this piece of shit!"

He slaps the side of the monitor. The woman in the children's corner gives us evils.

"Easy, old man. It's not a problem. I showed you, remember?"

"I remember a simpler time, Mars, that's what I remember."

I push the keys and the blue stock search screen comes back up. Dad groans. He's still in his dressing gown. "You're a genius."

"No, Dad, you're a caveman. Why are you even down here? Where's Diane?"

On cue, something bangs upstairs. Dad points up.

"Yeah. I'd better . . . You're good here, right?"

I nod. He goes upstairs.

The little girl lifts up the *Marvel Encyclopedia*. "Look, Mummy!"

The woman shakes her head. "No, Rosie, I said a proper book."

The girl puts the book back, frowning as she drags her feet over to where her mum is crouched in front of books for toddlers. Don't worry, Rosie, superheroes will still be there when you're old enough to choose.

Muffled shouts bleed through the ceiling. Another lovers' tiff.

I load up Roy Ayers on to the turntable and sit on the stool behind the till. Crackle. Chants. Bongos. I turn it down to background level. Saturdays are the best days. Full of possibility.

Blank pages, waiting to be scribbled on.

I imagine the counter is the control desk for a spaceship, the two front windows either side of the door my navigation screens. I'm the captain. I could go anywhere in the universe.

Where am I going? My mind's blank. Just a month ago my head was so full of stuff.

Stanley Milgram's (1963) obedience experiments. John Bowlby's Maternal Deprivation Hypothesis. The Loop of Henle and kidney function. The ambiguity of Iago's motivations.

All of it crammed in, facts and quotes and dates, loaded up, ready to regurgitate under exam conditions. Where is it all now? In a box tucked on to a shelf in the warehouse of my brain? Saved to the cloud?

I close my eyes and picture a pile of rubbish as big as a house, rough and jagged edges sticking out, but, instead of broken pieces of furniture and antique crap, it's just words, different-sized letters and sentences piled up on top of each other, a massive dark scribbled jumble of everything I've ever been taught. And I'm standing on the pavement in front of it, my hand reaching out, holding a lighter.

Think of Cara. Want to tell her. I reach into my bag for my phone and find my sketchbook. I don't remember putting it in here. Haven't taken it out of the house for ages.

You.

You put it in.

Someone stomps down the stairs and the moment is gone.

Diane's carrying a large navy-blue backpacker rucksack. Her face is flushed thunder.

I push my sketchbook out of sight.

The old man turns round, smiling, like he senses her presence. He's wearing a full suit, eager to impress. Diane doesn't even acknowledge him as she stomps over to me and drops her bag.

"Excuse me, Marcie," she says, taking the red strongbox from the shelf under the till.

"Are you OK?" I say, like a child.

She bangs the box on to the counter, then tips over the

old mug that holds the pens, fishing the key from a puddle of paperclips and drawing pins.

"I'm going to stay with my parents."

She opens the box and counts out a stack of notes. "Just what I'm owed," she says. I nod.

She gives me a sympathetic look, blows hair from her face, then waves her hand around like an untied balloon that's just been let go.

"Alton Towers has got nothing on that man, Marcie."

I glance at the door to upstairs. Why isn't he trying to stop her leaving? Did he give up?

"A rollercoaster's only fun because you know you're getting off at some point, right?" she says, folding the notes into her hip pocket. "Nobody wants a rollercoaster forever."

I'm supposed to say something. I can feel the old man watching from the shelves.

"When are you coming back?" I say.

Then she hugs me.

It's the first time she's ever done it and it's not the reserved, polite embrace I'd imagined it would be. It's the kind of firm, animal hug of an older sister who's going travelling and knows you'll be getting all the grief she would have got from your parents.

When she lets me go, we're both on the verge of tears.

"I'm sorry, Marcie." She picks up her bag and wipes her nose with her sleeve. "Oh, a guy phoned up and ordered a couple of books this morning. I don't remember his name, but it's on the system. He's picking them up on Tuesday."

"OK."

Diane looks at the doorway to the stairs.

"Look after him, OK? He needs you."

And there's another space for me to speak. But I don't.

I don't say, *Him? I can't even look after myself, Diane.*

I don't say, *My head is playing games with me right now.*

I don't say, *Please stay. He's been so much calmer since you've been around.*

I don't say anything. I don't even nod.

I just watch her leave and, as the shop door closes, I catch the broken look in the old man's eyes, like a young Bruce Wayne in that Gotham City alleyway.

Quiet with Dad has its own quality.

It's not like the painful tumbleweed wasteland it is with other people.

Growing up, I got used to him wandering off with a thought midway through a sentence and not looking back. Some new story idea that immediately superseded anything in the real world.

Sitting quietly with him while he stared out of the window, chewing over an idea, was as normal as watching TV.

This is different.

Watching him from the sofa, chin resting on his hands, he doesn't seem like he's lost in some plot point or character he's trying to grow. This feels like the stilted silence of a man digesting what has just happened. That thick silence that leaks out through the cracks of a mistake.

If there's one thing I think I've learned in my nearly eighteen years on this planet, it's that there is no situation the wrong words can't make worse. So I just sit with that double negative in my lap, staring across at the dormant fireplace.

Resting on the mantelpiece, in a cheap glass frame, is an A3, eight-panel, black-and-white comic strip. The first three panels are a creature that might be a bear, looking left, then right, then up. In the fourth panel, the bear looks at us and a speech bubble says, "Where Squirrel?" Five is him shrugging, six is him standing up, and in seven he turns around and half a squirrel is sticking out of his bum. Panel eight says "Lost Squirrel" by Marcie Baker. Age 7.

I laugh without meaning to. Dad looks over.

"Sorry," I say, covering my mouth.

"Don't be," he says, and the ten-ton mood lifts just enough for me to slip a question underneath.

"Will you call her?"

Dad looks at his hands.

"Happiness can exist only in acceptance."

"Dad?"

"Orwell. She's made her choice, Mars."

"What, and that's it?"

He shrugs. "It is what it is."

He glances at me, then goes back to the window. I swallow my frustration and just watch as the invisible elephant clomps into the room and plonks itself down in front of the fire, the word "MUM" painted in dripping red letters on its arse. I could say something. I want to.

But every sentence I run through in my head feels pointless.

Watching Dad like this, it's easy to remember he's a younger brother. The kind of boy who'd get escorted around by an older sister like Coral, taken to the playground, told not to wander off and pretty much left to his own devices. A boy who'd happily spend an entire afternoon inspecting leaves.

"Circles, Mars," he says after a while, stubbing out his cigarette. "What has happened will happen again."

"*Bullshit.*"

You're standing where the elephant was, bear arms folded in front of the fireplace.

"*Tell him that's bullshit.*" You're gesturing at me like a sports coach giving a pep talk.

"*Go on.*"

I shake my head, squeezing my eyes shut, willing you away.

"*I'm not leaving till you tell him*," you say.

I open my eyes.

"*Do it.*"

"Dad—"

"*Amor fati*, Mars," says Dad, starting on a new roll-up. "*Amor fati.*"

"*Do it, Marcie!*"

"Bullshit!"

You smile. I stand up. Dad drops his tobacco.

"The pitiful fortune-cookie lines I can just about handle, Dad, but when you start with the Latin . . . Get up."

"What?"

"*Tell him again.*"

"I said, get up! Get your shoes on: we're going out."

I walk over to him. Dad looks almost scared.

"I don't want to go out, Mars."

"I don't care what you want, Karl, we need air. This place stinks of self-pity."

I take his jacket off the hook next to the kitchen door and throw it at him.

"*Yes!*" you say. "*Go on, Marcie!*"

And I feel good. Better than good. I look at Dad.

"Come on. We're leaving."

☆

You're eleven.

It's the night before secondary school starts.

You're sitting at Coral's kitchen table with her and Dad. He's now living in a bedsit nearer town.

Coral's made curried goat and rice and peas. Dad compliments the food for the twenty-fifth time. Coral ignores him. She looks at you and asks what you have to say. The windows are all open, but there's still the faint smell of burnt polyester from the sofa.

You picture the green flames dancing as the paisley cushions ignited.

The light flickering in my smile.

You say you're sorry. That you were conducting a science experiment and it got out of control.

Coral stares at Dad.

Dad stares at his food.

You slide your hand into your pocket under the table and feel the smooth envelope, its edges worn almost furry from being held.

Coral tells your dad to say something. That it's getting ridiculous.

Your dad forces a smile and says a movie studio offered to buy the rights to *Dark Corners*. Coral asks how much. Dad says it doesn't matter: a book is a book, and a film is a film, they're not having it.

He raises his pineapple punch and says, "Screw Hollywood."

Coral looks at you, and rolls her eyes.

☆

"Thank you," says Dad as we walk back down the high street.

It's nearly six and everything is closed. A couple of hours' walking quietly through the park is as good as any therapy session.

I drop my used wet wipe in the bin outside the British Heart Foundation shop, belly full of chicken and chips.

"No problem."

We reach the shop and Dad starts patting his pockets.

"Maybe I should get a dog, with the park right there and everything?"

"Yeah? And who'll be the one who ends up walking him?" I say.

He fingers his bunch of keys for the right one. "Not you. You'll be gone."

"Dad . . ."

"Don't worry. I can handle myself." He holds up the shop door key proudly. "See?"

There's a sadness in his smile.

"Shall I come in for a bit?" I say. "I could wash up?"

"I'll be fine, Mars. Tell Coral I said hi."

He opens the door.

"I could come over tomorrow, cook you dinner?"

He shakes his head. "No need, Mars. You enjoy your Sunday off."

"I'll come on Monday then, help with the shop?"

I watch the realisation that Diane is gone sucker-punch him in the ribs. "Yeah. That'd be great."

He hands me his keys.

"OK then, call me if you need me, Dad, yeah?"

He nods an autopilot nod and closes the door.

You'll be gone.

I watch him through the glass. He looks older from behind, his body fading into shadow as he walks to the stairs.

Coral's wearing eyeliner.

"Oh, hey! I just sent you a message," she says, pointing back at the house. I can smell perfume.

"You look nice," I say.

She looks down at her outfit – navy-blue trouser suit, shimmery white top. "You think? Not too much?"

"Not at all. Who's the lucky guy?"

"Nobody special. Dom from work, you remember him? He came to my work birthday meal?"

She brushes fluff from her arm. The light dances in her perfectly cropped Lego hair.

"I won't be back late. Just a play and some food."

"A play?"

"Yeah, it's this Nigerian writer – she's written something – I don't know. Dom likes her work."

"But you hate the theatre."

"No I don't! Where'd you get that?"

"You said it."

She gives a sheepish grin. "Well, maybe it's time for a change."

Her nerves are cute. I imagine telling her, using the word "cute" to describe her, picture her face turning to rage and the carnage that would follow. "Cute" is one of Coral's red-rag words.

"Well, have fun," I say.

"Thanks, sweetie. You OK?"

"Yeah. Fine."

"How's my little brother?"

Picture Dad shuffling back to the stairs.

"Who knows?"

"Not me, Mars. We could all get lost forever in the right side of Karl Baker's brain."

"I think I'm going to help in the shop from Monday."

"OK, save some extra money, good thinking."

"Yeah. Dad's busy with the book."

Coral smiles and squeezes my shoulder. "Course he is." She checks her purse for her phone. "I left a twenty on the kitchen table in case you wanted to order food, OK?"

"Thanks."

"All right. Text me if you need to. I'll be home by midnight."

As she reaches the gate, she gives a nervous wave.

I wave back, feeling like a parent watching her only child leave for prom.

Shoes off. Laptop to the lounge. Connect Bluetooth to the stereo.

YouTube. Chance The Rapper – *Acid Rap* (Full Mixtape).

Skip ad. Volume up to thirty.

Slippers and house hoodie on.

Slide-dance to the kitchen. Freezer. Cookies and Cream Häagen-Dazs and ice cubes.

Blueberries and milk from the fridge. Banana from the bowl.

The growl of the blender. Get my old curly straw from the drawer. Detach the jug.

Open the back door. Lean on the wall and take a deep breath of dusk.

Drop my straw in and drink.

Cold and sweet.

I'm good.

"Course you are."

I smile into my milkshake.

"You took your time."

"Yeah, well. Not all of us have nothing to do."

I turn round.

"Got a lot on, have you?"

"Yes, actually."

Stare-off. Loser blinks first. Twista is speed-rapping from the other room. I see a small tick-shaped scar on the bridge of your nose. My dry eyeballs sting. You keep staring. Can't hold it. Can't hold it.

Blink.

"Ha! Still undefeated!"

"Shut up, Bearboy."

"You shut up, Fartsy."

Then we laugh.

And something inside me unwinds.

☆

Sitting in your garden, waiting for the dark.

One of Coral's deep-red scented candles burns safe in its fish-bowl glass. Some kind of bird is singing and the music from inside feels far away.

Me and you, Marcie.

Bliss.

"You know this is stupid, right?"

You don't look at me as you say it, staring down the narrow garden. The dead apple tree sprouting out of the ground looks like a gnarled witch's finger pointing at the sky.

"I'm nearly eighteen, Thor."

I choose my words carefully, wary of bursting this bubble.

"*Maybe being alone is stupid.*"

You don't reply. Have I ruined it?

"I'm not alone, Thor."

The flickering flame in your eyes. My stupid mouth.

"I have people. Friends."

I'm such an idiot.

"*I know,*" I say, looking down.

The bird stops singing just as the track from inside finishes. Quiet.

I won't say anything else. I'll just be here. Let me stay. Please.

Then you smile. "Not like you though."

And my heart swells.

You reach your hand out. To me.

I lay my paw on top, feel your fingertips on my pads. My Marcie.

"No more dares though, Thor. OK? No more trouble."

I nod.

And, right now, that feels like enough.

*

The six-train carriage is empty. It's gone midnight.

Cutting through the night on its high track, it feels like I'm riding in the dark, graffitied belly of some massive metal worm.

Left you asleep on the sofa when I heard Coral's key in the door. The end credits of *Blade* rolling up the TV screen. Still the best comic book to film adaptation ever. All this hype about Deadpool. Never liked him. Talks too much.

My reflection smiles in the dark glass.

Blue.

Shit.

We had plans. I completely forgot.

Idiot.

She'll be mad. Should call her. Will call her.

But I won't.

Feels like there's no time.

The world turns quicker when you have a purpose. That sounds like a Leyland line.

Maybe some of his sensei persona is rubbing off.

The fade is coming.

I have to be clever. I'll start with the roof,

take that off first. If I rig the supports for the walls, that could take a couple of days. I'll do the job, just really slowly. If anyone asks, I'm being careful. Precise. Respecting my craft. Keeping your bedroom door safe.

My passage to you.

SUNDAY

(10 DAYS LEFT)

THOR BAKER:
FADE COUNSELLING SESSION 2

8AM

You seem different.

What does that mean?

I'm not sure. Lighter.

I don't know what you're talking about.

Has something happened?

Like what?

I don't know. Something good?

Alan, I'm sitting here at eight o'clock on a Sunday morning when I could be in bed, watching *Freaks and Geeks*, eating leftover chicken. What's good about that?

You can talk to me you know? The reason you're here is to tell me things.

I've got nothing to tell.

I see. What about the house?

What did you say?

The house. Marcie's house?

How do you know about that?

Do I really need to answer that?

Are you spying on me?

Should I be?

Who do you think you are?

Thor, please.

Who was it? Someone from the train?

What train? Thor, sit down.

I don't have to listen to you.

I'm afraid you do, Thor.

Says you. What the hell?

I'd like you to sit down.

What are you doing? How are you . . .? My legs, I can't move my legs!

Thor . . .

It hurts.

Thor . . .

Stop!

So sit down. Thank you.

How did you do that?

We all have our gifts.

It felt like my legs . . . I couldn't control them.

You don't need to fight me, Thor.

No shit.

I'm sorry I did that. I don't want things to be that way.

What, you mean treating me like a prisoner?

Thor, please calm down. I don't want us to fight. This is a very important time for you and my job is to help you process it.

By forcing me to sit down?

No, by listening. Nothing you say in this room will go any further. It's just between us. No judgements.

Don't do that again, Alan.

I won't, I promise. I just want us to talk.

I could get to you, you know? Before you even think whatever it is you think to make that happen. I'm quick. I could be over this desk and on you before you blink.

I don't doubt it, Thor.

I'll scratch your face off.

I understand. Now shall we talk about the house?

About the door?

I don't know what to say.

How did it feel, stepping through after all this time?

I don't know.

Can you try and describe it? Did it feel good? Did it feel right?

It felt like coming home.

☆

"I swear you were born in the wrong decade."

Cara turns off the engine. It's nearly half seven and we're in the car park across the road from the Black Lion.

"You and my brother don't even deserve mobile phones." She's only half joking.

"Has Morgan gone back to uni?" I say.

Cara checks her face in the rear-view mirror. "He was still in his room when I left. Probably holding out for a lift from Dad. Loser."

"How is he?"

"How the hell should I know? Haven't seen him once all weekend. He's like a hermit crab."

She neatens the edge of her lipstick with her finger and licks her top teeth. "That'll have to do."

"You look great, Car."

"You have to say that. That's why I keep you around." She flashes me a smile. "Grab the stuff."

"I just don't see why we have to film it," I say, picking up her camera and the tripod from between my feet. Outside the pub there's already a small crowd of art-student-looking characters on the patio area, drinking and smoking and no doubt competing with each other over who has the best knowledge of Alt-J B-sides.

"I hate stuff like this," I say, closing my door. "People who call themselves 'artists' are always full of it."

"Oh, shut up, will you? That's not even what you think. Your dad's an artist."

"Yeah, I know."

Cara rolls her eyes. "Check the memory card. We're here to support him. You know he cares what you think."

"I know you care what he thinks."

Cara's gives me the middle finger. "I know I don't give a shit about what you think I care about what he thinks, bitch."

And I can't stop myself laughing.

The room is through the back of the pub, up some stairs that smell like toilets.

We walk in to an old Motown-sounding song I don't recognise.

A blonde girl behind a little table with too much glitter around her eyes ticks our name off Sean's guest list and stamps the back of our hands with little red hearts.

The place is half full of people sitting and standing around, waiting for the night to start.

I watch Cara scan the dimly lit room. She points to the back left corner behind the rows of chairs, next to the low DJ booth.

"You set up there. I'll get some roaming stuff on my phone. Do you want a drink?"

"Not really."

"Have something – you'll look weird otherwise."

"Fine, get me whatever you're having."

She goes to the bar. I don't see Sean as I go to my designated spot.

People seem impressed by the fact that I'm carrying a camera, nodding at me like I must be important. Guess that's part of the appeal.

There are two mics on stands on the small corner stage,

lit by one warm spotlight. It's actually a pretty nice room. Almost feels like we're in someone's house, with a bunch of strangers.

The girl at the decks has a topknot and nose ring. She looks at the gear in my hands and nods her approval. I start setting up the tripod and spot Sean, over by the stage, talking to an older guy wearing a dark flat cap. He sees me and raises a thumb, saying something to the guy, then heading my way.

"You made it!"

His smile makes him look stoned. He's holding a bottle of beer by the neck, fresh white T-shirt against the dark of his arms.

"Course," I say, sliding the camera into the tripod saddle. "How you feeling?"

Sean nods, reassuring himself. "Yeah. Good. We're on in the second half. Nice T."

I look down at MF DOOM's masked face on my T-shirt.

"Thanks."

"Thanks for filming it, man. That looks expensive."

"It's Cara's. She's directing."

We both look over to the bar, where Cara is explaining

something to the scruffy guy serving drinks. I watch Sean's eyes on her as he swigs from his bottle.

"I hope you like it, Mars," he says.

"I'm sure I will."

"We're still working on the live set, but Ben's pretty sick on the sampler."

"Cool."

"I was actually thinking, you know, about asking you to do something?"

His face goes sheepish. "I thought maybe, for the EP, you'd do some, you know, some artwork? One of your sketches?"

I can see the tiniest edge of the scar at the neck of his T-shirt, and I try not to picture his chest underneath, the stretched glossy patch of the skin graft.

"I don't really draw any more. Haven't for ages. I'm not—"

"Course. Yeah. No worries. Just asking. How's your dad?"

"Still Dad."

We share the same knowing smile.

"Yo, you should come by mine one time," he says, playfully batting my arm. "I'll play you some tracks. Nan'll cook a banquet if I tell her you're coming. It's been too long, Mars."

I nod too much. "Yeah. Sounds good. Let's try and find time."

"Yeah. Let's do it. I'll catch you after, yeah?"

And he walks off, meeting Cara on her way over with two drinks. They exchange a few words, then he carries on to the front.

"Man, I wish I could read that boy," Cara says, handing me a glass of Coke. "Hot and cold, hot and cold. He's like a frigging radiator. Did he say anything about me?"

"Calm down, will you?" I say.

Cara sips her drink and shakes her head. "I'm an idiot. Why am I such an idiot, Mars?"

"Why are you an idiot?"

The place is filling up, people taking seats, an excited energy in the room.

"I told him he looked like Kano. Why did I do that? Of all the things I could've said . . ."

I stop myself from giggling by taking a sip. Diluted cola sugar.

"He does though," I say, putting my drink down on the shelf behind me, "and it's a compliment."

"Nothing's gonna happen anyway. I need to let it go." She twists her necklace and strokes the smooth well of her collarbone. "Promise me something, Mars. When we get to uni, if I meet someone, don't let me be this lame, OK?"

"You're not lame. It's just not the right time."

She's not really listening to me though, her eyes flitting round the room, stealing glances of him by the stage.

"He's not on till the second half, Car. I might go get some food."

"No! Stay. Film everything, then I can cut something cool together."

"Are you serious?"

People start to go quiet as the music fades down and a pasty boy in a trilby and waistcoat steps on to the stage. Cara rolls her eyes, and we both muffle our laughter as the house lights go down.

Cold air kisses the sweat off my neck.

Circles of people are gathered outside the pub under the fuzzy, post-gig spotlights of the patio lamps. Sean's smoking in the middle of four girls looking up at him like he's Jesus. There's weed in the air.

"I need a cigarette," says Cara, next to me.

"You don't smoke, Car," I say, double-checking I've not left anything upstairs.

"Maybe I do. Maybe University Cara is a roll-ups and whisky kind of girl."

Her eyes are on Sean and his fawning audience. I bump her with my elbow.

"Make sure you get a brown satchel and a dog-eared copy of *On the Road* to carry around with you too. Where are you going? Don't leave me!"

She smiles back at me as she walks over to Sean and the girls. Sean splits two of the others with his arm, making space for her in the circle. He glances over at me, as Cara fake smiles at her competitors, and something tells me to back her up, go over and help her talk hip hop, but the sad desperation of the situation keeps my back pinned to the wall.

Across the street the chip shop glows like a white-tiled oasis. I'm not even that hungry, but food will get me out of this sorry scene.

"You a DOOM fan then?"

The topknot DJ girl is blatantly smoking a spliff. She's shorter than she looked in her booth; younger. Maybe a year or two older than us and it's pretty obvious that she's a clean girl trying to look dirty rather than the other way round.

"Yeah," I say. "You?"

"Big time!" she says through a mouthful of smoke, then holds out her joint.

"I'm good, thanks."

"Yeah, course, whatever, man. You know my cousin met him one time."

I pull the interested expression she's hoping for to carry on. "Yeah. He was DJ for his opening act, down in London, forget the name of the place. You're Marcie, right?" She holds out her hand. "I'm Rumer."

You're not here but I hear your voice. "*Course you are*."

As I shake her dry fingers, I notice the end of a sentence tattooed on the inside of her elbow.

"It's a quote," she says, sliding up her T-shirt to show the full line. I squint to read the joined-up letters. "Don't play what's there, play what's not there."

And something about the line completely cracks my perception. I like the words. I wasn't supposed to like them. She's not supposed to offer anything that affects me. It's too cool to be on her arm, or maybe she's cooler than

I let her seem, or maybe, after standing through a whole night of people up on stage spouting melodramatic crap, convinced they're changing the world, it's nice to hear a simple, succinct sentence.

"Who said it?"

"Miles Davis."

I nod like I know all about Miles Davis, his back catalogue, his personal story, his cultural impact. Not just his name.

"What did you think then?" says Rumer. "You enjoy the night?"

"Yeah. It was good."

I look over to Cara. Her and the other girls all have their heads tilted back in laughter like Sean just said the funniest thing ever uttered by a human being.

"I can't stand most of it, to be honest," Rumer says, shrugging guiltily. "I just like the chance to play a set, even a shitty little pre-show one."

The honesty of her comment throws me off. This girl's not what I made her, and I can't quite work out whether I'm safe to say what I really think or if I should stay non-committal.

"Me either," I say, feeling the release of the truth.

Rumer relights her joint, rotating it so it burns evenly. "It's like having to listen to the diaries of people whose diaries you would never want to read."

"Exactly!" I say.

We both nod, smiling together, and for a second I almost reach for the joint.

"Look at them, crowded round him like pigeons." She points over at Sean and the girls. "You not interested?"

I shrug.

"Got your eye on someone else?"

We both look at Cara, and it's suddenly like she's too close. This stranger. I take a side step away from her. She doesn't seem to notice.

"He's good though, eh?" she says, still looking at Sean.

Three of the other girls are walking away, bowing out of the race, leaving just Cara and a girl in rolled-up dungarees and box-fresh black Huaraches.

"He's all right," I say.

"Says you're a sick artist."

"What?"

Rumer nods. "Comic stuff he said. Like, drawings and that. Is that your thing then?"

Sean's bedroom. Year Seven. Me on his floor sketching

him while he rhymes into an Afro comb in the mirror. The two of us crying with laughter.

"He doesn't know what he's talking about."

"So you're not an artist?"

The tone in her voice is too knowing. I throw the tripod strap over my shoulder and tuck the camera case under my arm.

"Not at all."

MONDAY

(9 DAYS LEFT)

Letting myself into the shop feels good. Like this place could be mine.

There are a couple of bills and a brown, book-sized package on the mat.

I lock the door behind me and drop the post on the counter. A flicker and a ping as the old strip lights blink into life. Full shelves feel like the warm walls of a den.

Bookshops rule.

Funny how some people think of books as torture, and some of us see them as gifts. Maybe it's genetic? Maybe it's upbringing? Nature. Nurture. Coral would have ideas.

I'd be lying if I said there wasn't any kind of ego-driven, intellectual satisfaction from being surrounded by hundreds of stories. There's a definite sense of self-importance, of feeling like I own them all, and that my brain is richer for it, but it's more than that. Underneath the self-congratulation of feeling clever, there's a much simpler connection.

A feeling of comfort and safety.

And choice.

Like I could go anywhere I wanted, whenever I want. Or just go nowhere at all.

I load up *Motown Classics* on to the turntable and give Johnny Cash gun fingers on my way to the stairs.

The little room that was a snowdrift is weirdly tidy. Just a couple of boxes of printer paper in the corner.

"Dad?"

He's not in the living room.

There's two empty bottles of red wine and at least ten balls of scrunched-up legal-pad paper on the table. The jagged glass ashtray is overflowing.

"Dad?"

The kitchen is as clean as it can be. Empty sink. Draining board wiped down.

I walk back through the little room, across the tiny landing to Dad's bedroom door, and knock.

"Dad? It's Marcie. You up?" I hear stirring inside.

"I'll make coffee, yeah?"

"Morning, gorgeous."

His hair is still wet from the shower, cheeks shiny from a shave.

I point to the coffee on the table, the wine bottles and paper balls cleared away.

"Thanks, Mars," he sits down. "What time is it?"

"It's just after nine. You OK?"

He takes a mouthful of coffee and closes his eyes, waiting for the caffeine to reach the tips of his nerves.

"Dad?"

"I'm fine. Got a meeting."

"Yeah? With who?"

"Oscar's arranged a lunch with some lady from Picador."

"Oscar, your agent Oscar? That's great! About the new book?"

Dad nods. "She's getting the train up from London. They publish DeLillo. Have you seen my tobacco?"

I pick up the pouch from the coffee table and take it over to him.

"That's exciting, right? Did they read some pages?"

"What pages?" he says, starting to roll up.

I touch his shoulder. "Good to start a dialogue though? Nice that they're interested."

Dad forces a smile. "Yeah." He sparks his cigarette. "Enough of my nonsense, how are you? How's freedom suiting you?"

"Dunno." I go back to the sofa and sit down. "I was thinking I could get Cara to help out in the shop. I reckon between us we can handle it. Give you time to write."

"I don't think so, Mars. You should be off enjoying your summer, not holed up in a dusty old shop. I'll find someone, don't worry."

I don't feel like an argument, so I don't remind him that the only reason he even met Diane was because she came to a reading he did and, since he refused to do any more readings more than two years ago, combined with the fact that he has the social skills of an ironing board, the chances of him actually meeting a prospective employee are pretty slim. As is often the case with Dad, the best thing to do is agree, wait for him to forget he even said anything and then do what you want anyway.

"OK," I say, finishing my coffee, "just until you find someone then."

The back room looks like a museum installation of a nuclear bunker.

Even standing up, all I can see through the high strip of window is the dark top of the tree across the back alleyway. The naked light bulb hanging from its thin white cord in the middle of the ceiling looks like some forlorn Victorian attempt at fibre optics. An old schoolteacher's desk pushed under the window has a line of books against the wall and one of those lamps shaped like a drooping, frosted-glass tulip. The sculpted pine chair underneath it has wheels and looks like it might recline.

In the far corner, an old beige-and-brown filing cabinet acts as the headboard to a low single cot bed that hasn't been slept in for a while. At the bottom of the bed, a battered brown two-seater leather sofa looks like it was plucked from a skip. The walls are empty and grey.

It's perfect.

Apart from the books, and a faint hint of sunflowers,

there's no trace of Diane. It makes me think of Richard McGuire's graphic novel *Here*. A space occupied and left and occupied again.

"It's probably haunted."

You're leaning against the wall at the foot of the bed, red Charizard T-shirt hugging your muscular chest.

"Any place that's empty and neat is usually haunted."

"Says who?"

"It's common knowledge. Ghosts don't like mess."

"Shut up."

You sit down on the edge of the bed. "I'm just saying. You won't catch me sleeping in here."

"And where do you sleep?"

You shake your head.

"So your stupid rules still apply then?"

"Afraid so."

"So no questions about where you go?"

You shake you head again.

"Convenient," I say, stroking the cool wall.

"Hardly. This is a surprise for me too, you know."

I drop my bag on the desk and lean on the wall opposite you.

"I'm not crazy, Thor."

You frown deeply. "Neither am I."

You stand up, like you're ready to fight. Your head almost touches the light bulb.

"Shall I go?" you say.

If the crown prince of Asgard and Ororo Munroe had a son, that's what you look like. Except for the bear arms.

"No. Stay."

Your smile makes all my questions disappear. You point at my bag.

"Sketchbook in there?"

"Why don't you tell me?"

You wait for me to say more. I don't.

"Fine."

Then you start walking out of the room.

"Where are you going?"

"Where do you think? We've got a shop to open."

☆

One old guy, dressed like he came straight from a funeral, is the only person who comes in all morning. He shuffles around, checking over his shoulder every so often, like he's waiting for someone. It would be creepy if he wasn't so old.

You ask him if he needs help finding something and at first he is cagey, like he speaks a different language, then your smile wins him over. Watching you help him, answering his fifty questions, taking books down for him, you look happy. Like you fit in the picture.

I'm so bored.

I try not to fidget, or make it obvious, but by midday I'm ready to rip every single book off every single shelf just to make something happen.

Your dad comes downstairs looking like someone dressed him up for a job interview.

"I'm off," he says to you.

I laugh from the children's corner. "*You got that right, Karl. Way off.*"

You cut me evils, then go over and straighten his collar.

"Hope it goes well," you say, picking fluff out of his hair.

"And you'll be fine here on your own?"

"*She's not on her own, Karl,*" I say.

You don't even look at me as you walk him to the door. "I'll be fine, Dad."

"I should only be a couple of hours. Unless they smell a rat early."

"Stop it," you say, kissing him on the cheek.

He's lucky to have you.

"*Lock it.*"

"What?"

"*Lock the door. Flip the sign.*"

You're doubtful. "No."

"*Come on. It's lunchtime. People have to eat, don't they?*" I walk over to the till.

"What are you doing, Thor?"

"*Shut up. Is it locked?*"

I find a familiar record in the stack of vinyl. You lock the door and walk over as the piccolo intro starts. I turn the volume up as far as it will go. The acoustics of the shop are amazing, something about the books maybe. Leyland would love it.

"*You remember this?*"

I jump over the counter and take your hands.

"No stopping till the record's done, remember?"

And your smile tells me you do.

☆

Surrounded by books, we dance.

Smokey Robinson and the Miracles' "Tears of a Clown" turned up full on the stereo and there's something about the room, the low ceiling, blinds pulled down in the windows, the music running round the shelves. It's like a dream.

You swing my arms, then let me go and spin off around the display tables, your eyes closed, bear arms stretched out like one of those giant helicopter seeds that fall from tall trees. I've got my hands in my hoodie pockets, pushed out like wings, swinging my hips, surfing the floor, and everything else has fallen away.

The song finishes. Another starts. We dance on. Beaming like babies.

Let's just do this.

Let's stay here.

Everything else is so serious. Everything else is so pressured.

The song starts to fade.

You open your eyes and see me watching you. I wave. You go to wave back, but wobble. You try to steady yourself, but your dizzy momentum carries you into the film and music shelves and you fall back. The crash sends books tumbling down over your shoulders as you land on your backside, still looking at me. And I laugh so hard I almost pee.

You pick up a hardback that fell into your lap and start reading it like you planned the whole thing. I sit down next to you in the puddle of books, our backs against the half-empty shelves.

The record ends and there's the mechanical sound of the needle loading itself back into its cradle and then the shop is quiet, except for our breathing.

"What you reading there, Mr Baker?"

"This?" You hold it up. "I'm glad you asked, Miss Baker. This is my first novel. I like to read my old work from time to time, just to get perspective, you know? It's part of my 'process'."

"I see. It's been a while since the novel was published, and we've had no new work from you in the years since. Would you say that you have perhaps been experiencing somewhat of a writer's block?"

You nod, deadpan. "Some inexperienced outsiders might argue that, yes, although, as my first writing mentor always said to me, 'Greatness is a mule that will not be rushed.'"

I bite my lip to keep from laughing.

"Wow. That's very profound."

"I know." You hold up a paw. "Of course, with claws, it does take me nearly a day to type a sentence."

I'm going to burst.

"Indeed. And can I ask what it is you're working on right now?"

"Well, I don't want to give too much away, but my new work which, I have to say, may be my most stunning to date, is shaping up to be a terrifically complex opus, something of a kind of post-dystopian, pseudo-utopian, erm . . ."

"Fallopian?"

And the roar of our laughter fills the shop. We are in our bubble. Together.

You wipe your eyes with the back of your paw.

"Let's order pizza," I say.

But you're looking at your paw, frowning.

"Thor, what's wrong?"

You stare at your paw, opening and closing your fist.

"Thor?"

"I have to go, Marcie."

"What?"

"I have to go."

"Go where? Why?"

You look at me.

"I'm sorry."

"Where've you been?"

"I had a meeting."

"I know you had a meeting – at lunchtime. It's nearly half five, Dad."

"Is it?"

"So it went well then?"

"Waste of time."

"How come?"

"Errand boys, sent by grocery clerks, Mars. That's all they are. I don't know what Oscar was thinking."

"What does that mean? They didn't like the story idea? Dad?"

"I don't need them."

"Will you meet another publisher?"

Dad looks round the shop. "How've you been? Busy?"

"Not exactly."

"That's good."

"Dad, are you OK?"

"I'm tired. I'm going to go upstairs."

"OK. Shall I make you some dinner? Are you hungry? I could go get chicken?"

"No thanks."

"We could watch a film? Something old. *Harvey*?"

"Not today, Mars. I think I might just read a while, then sleep."

"All right then, so I'll see you tomorrow?"

"Yeah. Tomorrow."

"OK."

"Thank you, for today, watching the shop. Big help."

"No problem, Dad. I'm happy to."

☆

Light cuts through the dust on to my face.

I push the underlay and broken tiles out on to the roof. The scraping sound of them sliding down, the silence as they fall through the air, then the crash as they hit the ground out in front of the house. So satisfying. Adjust my feet and punch again.

You didn't want me to go. I could feel it. The magic of it. The guilt.

Have to be careful.

Nine days left.

Knocking off the front of the roof means if anyone comes to inspect, they'll see I've started. If I rig the wall supports today too, I can say that it was a longer job than I thought it would be. Old brickwork.

Who am I kidding?

What am I doing?

This can't end well.

Won't.

Truth hurts.

Standing on the attic beam, I push off enough gauze and insulation to stick my head out.

I can see all the way back to the city. A tapestry of weird and wonderful creatures. A collage of functional structures and unbelievable buildings, twinkling in the last rays of the fading sun.

I try to work out which tower block is mine, but, from this far away, they all look the same.

Being high up in the daytime feels different than it does at night. At night, it feels like a zooming-in, like the focus of everything is narrowing in on you, but in the day it's more like moving out to a panoramic wide shot, and you can feel just how small a dot you are on the planet.

I'm struck by the vastness of the sky.

I wish you could see this place, Marcie.

I wish it worked both ways.

We could sit on the broken roof of your house, throwing tiles into the street until the sun goes down.

It's nearly dark when I get back to the block. The deep red of the lobby carpet is a dance floor.

I stretch out my arms and spin as though I'm dancing. With you. Oh, Marcie.

The lift doors open and Blue is there.

I don't know where to look.

"Lame, Baker. Just lame."

"I'm so sorry. I got caught up."

"Whatever." She steps out, pushing past me into the lobby.

"Blue, wait. I was *going* to call, I swear, I just . . . when I'm smashing, I lose track of time. I didn't. I'm sorry."

"I won't let you make me play the whiny, desperate girl, Thor."

"I'm not. I promise. This is my fault. Wait, were you upstairs?"

"Yeah. I just left a note."

"Saying what?"

"Saying *fuck you, Thor*, that's what. Don't make plans if you're not going to see them through. I came. I waited. Nothing. And you couldn't even call, all of yesterday?"

She goes to walk away. I grab her arm. She looks down at my paw on her and waits for me to let go. We both know she could tear me in half if she wanted to.

"I'm sorry, Blue. Really I am."

She pulls her arm away.

"Good. Go be sorry by yourself."

TUESDAY

(8 DAYS LEFT)

I can smell smoky bacon and coffee as I come down the stairs.

Coral usually has a breakfast smoothie on a weekday and she doesn't drink coffee.

Bacon and coffee means it's either my birthday or bad news.

It's not my birthday.

"Morning, Marcie. Hungry?"

He looks like Nick Fury. Minus the eyepatch. His head is shiny smooth and he's got the body of an army general, older, but still coiled for action. And he's wearing Coral's dressing gown.

A stranger in the kitchen feels weird. A stranger in the kitchen wearing Coral's dressing gown, holding our frying pan, using my name, is just plain awkward.

"I'm Dom," he says, holding out his free hand. "We met briefly once. I work with your aunt at the university."

I wrap my cardigan tighter around my body and we shake.

"Coral's in the shower," he says, then just gets back on with preparing breakfast like it's the most natural thing in the world. The way he moves around as if everything is completely familiar takes the edge off the awkward and I sit down.

"Coffee?" he says, like a flight attendant.

"Yes, please."

He pours me a mug.

"Sorry for the surprise appearance. We ended up having a drink last night and shared a taxi. Milk?"

His voice sounds a bit like the automated cashier recording at the post office.

Till number four, please.

"No, thanks."

He hands me the mug and starts whisking eggs.

"Do you think she'd prefer an omelette, or scrambled?"

"Scrambled," I say. "But make sure they're well done. She hates them runny."

He turns round and gives me a wink. "Thanks."

And I like him. Just like that. That's how my brain works. It only needs a minute.

"She doesn't drink coffee though," I say.

Dom stops whisking. "No?"

I shake my head. "Makes her sick. Chocolate too."

Dom's face screws up. "No coffee or chocolate? What kind of creature is she?"

I smile.

"The kind that loves fresh orange juice." I point to the cupboard next to the sink.

"Juicer's in there." And I wink, because what the hell? I can wink if I want to.

☆

THOR BAKER:
FADE COUNSELLING SESSION 3
8AM

You look tired.

Late night.

In the real?

No. The park. Doesn't matter.

OK. Let's talk about what happened.

When?

When she sent you away.

Jeez, jump right in, why don't you?

Time is of the essence, Thor.

Fine. What about it?

All of it.

All of it?

Yes.

Were *you* sent away?

I think it's better if I ask the questions.

You were, weren't you? That's why you're allowed to do this, I mean apart from the cliché beard and polo neck?

I've trained, Thor. I wasn't "allowed".

So you've sat here then?

No.

You didn't have to?

Not in this room.

Somewhere else?

Yes. Now can we get back to you? Let's go back six years. Tell me what happened.

You know what happened. It's all in the file.

Yes, but, like I've explained, the point is me hearing it from you. How you see it, what you remember.

Like I could forget?

Thor . . .

Like I could just put what happened in a box on a shelf somewhere and get on with my life?

Thor, listen . . .

Is that what you did, Alan? Did you just forget?

Eight days.

What?

You have eight days. Until the fade.

So?

So, it might be worth making better use of our time together if you want to transition well.

You mean if I want to make sure I'm not standing in the park, screaming at the sky?

Yes, if that's how you want to put it. I can help, Thor. Tell me what happened, and we'll go from there, OK?

How come you're fine with it, with me crossing over?

Because I trust you.

You hardly know me.

I know you better than you think. And I know that you'll do what's right when it's time.

What does it feel like, I mean, the actual moment?

Everyone experiences it differently. And it's less a moment and more a process. Separating from the mind that made you is complicated.

It's crazy really, when you think about it. Isn't it?

I can't argue with that, Thor. But it's the way it's always been. And one thing I can say is that preparation will make it easier. I can vouch for that.

And knocking down the house is part of it? My final test?

Yes.

Will knocking it down make things easier?

No. Just clearer.

Still hurts though, doesn't it?

Yes, Thor. It does.

☆

I close the front door and the narrow hallway falls into shadow. Breathe in memories, and stare at the stairs. Stare at the stairs. Homophone.

I'm standing right here. Before.

I'm standing right here, calling after you as you run up these stairs. You're eleven, and angry. Some girls caught you drawing in the library at lunchtime. Hunched over your sketchbook, lost in your art, you didn't see them circling you. A snarling gang of other Year Seven girls who already know each other and think they run things. You tried to hide your picture, but they got it. Laughing. Cara wasn't there. You haven't become friends yet. Sean was out in the cages playing football.

You told me not to come when you're at school.

I should've been there, Marcie.

Walking home, you wouldn't tell me what they said. What you were drawing. I pushed and pushed. Asked if it was about your mum. Told you I would get them. You got angry. You started running. I ran too, but I couldn't catch up.

I stretch out my right arm and drag my claws up the wall as I climb the stairs.

The short landing is as dark as it always was.

Bathroom on the left. Coral's door at the end, the empty box room adjacent.

I reach your door.

There was a poster. Somebody in a mask. What

was it? Just the bare white paint now. A couple of centimetres of wood between here and there.

Here and you.

I can feel the regular drop kick of my heartbeat.

How can I destroy this place?

Eight days.

Because I have to.

Starting now.

Then a noise from inside.

I hear it. Clear as a bell.

My name.

☆

"Morning!"

Dad slides out of the kitchen and I almost jump out of my skin.

He's holding a new cafetière full of coffee in one hand and a white mug in the other.

"Why would you do that?" I press my chest and feel my heart kicking.

"Good for the blood," he says, tapping his head with the mug. "Remember?"

He's wearing an open white shirt over his white vest and he has shoes on.

"Have you been out?"

"No point moping, Mars. Time to smack the day on the arse with a banjo."

"What?"

He holds up the coffee. "I went to that new organic place by the optician's. Columbian. High-end."

"OK, doc. Is this where you tell me all about the flux capacitor?"

Dad spins round, puts the coffee and mug down on the table, spins back and grabs me by the shoulders.

"I had a thought. Last night, in bed."

"That's great, Dad. For the story?"

He shakes his head, eyes wide. "You don't make it rain by staring at the sky, Marcie."

"OK..."

He squeezes my shoulders. "No more staring. I'll see you downstairs."

"What, you're opening the shop?"

He gives a wide-eyed nod.

"But it's not even half nine, Dad. We don't open until ten."

But he's already off, striding to the stairs like a hunter heading into the woods.

I go to the table and sniff the cafetière. Somewhere else in the country, somewhere green, right now, Diane is sitting in her parents' conservatory, sipping a coffee with her broadsheet paper.

I pour myself some of Dad's high-end Columbian and raise my mug.

"To Alton Towers."

I lean back in the wooden swivel chair. The high-end Columbian has got my brain feeling like a pinball machine. Through the high strip of window, the sky is tropical-ocean blue.

I swivel round and look at the doorway. The tumbling piano of Philip Glass coming from the shop. This won't last. Sooner or later Dad will need me.

I feel like a private investigator waiting for a call.

MARCIE BAKER P.I.

NO CASE IS TOO SMALL.

IN FACT, SMALL CASES ARE BETTER.

LESS WORK.

I put my hands behind my head like I'm sunbathing.

From the second she walked in, I knew she was trouble, see?

Five ten, expensive fur coat, lips the colour of fresh blood and hands like a lumberjack.

I lean further back in the chair and mime smoking a cigarette.

She looked at me like I was something she just scraped off her Jimmy Choo. "You don't look like much, Marcie Baker," she said, peeling off her coat to reveal a Coke-bottle body wrapped in a pure white dress.

"Yeah, well," I said, pulling on my cigarette, "last chances don't have to."

I put my feet up on the desk. I'd make a brilliant private investigator. There should be a degree course for that. The chair wobbles, and I try to straighten up, but it's too late; the wheels squeak, the seat squeezes forward and I fall flat on my back.

Pain spreads down through the base of my spine into my hips. Thousands of tiny nerve endings running screaming down the inside of my thighs like One Direction fans trying to get to the front of the stage. You make your own bed, and then you lie in it.

From this position, I can see the light caught in the cobwebs where the wall meets the ceiling. You should be here. Laughing at me. "Where are you, Thor Baker?"

"I'm here."

You look down at me. "You're on the floor."

"I know that."

You nod, then lie down next to me. Piano from the shop. The faint tap of the computer keyboard.

"How is he?"

"I have no idea."

"Enigma."

"What?"

"You taught me that word. You were drawing a monster sidekick. We were in your room. You said it was a killer rhino shark. I said, wouldn't that mean he would just kill you? You said no, that he was nice to you, but deadly to everyone else. You said he was an enigma."

"When was that?"

"You were nine. It was a Sunday."

"You remember that?"

"I remember it all."

I sit up.

You do the same.

"What's wrong, Marcie?"

"I don't know . . . I'm fine, I guess."

Then you smack my knee. "Fuck fine!"

I cackle like an old woman.

"What's funny?"

"Fuck fine?"

You look offended. "That's what I said. What, I can't swear?"

"Guess so."

"I had puberty too, you know."

"Good for you."

You jump up on to your feet like a surfer catching a wave. "So fuckety, fuck fine! Fine will quietly fucking kill you, like a fucking gas leak." You point at the filing cabinet. "What the fuck's in there?"

"Boring!"

I duck as something red flies past me.

"Watch it!"

An A4 accounts log book smacks against the wall behind me and drops to the floor.

"What's the point of a drawer with nothing in it?" you say, opening the second one down and rummaging inside. Typed pages and legal-looking documents start raining around me as you fling them.

"Thor! Stop it!"

"Aha!" you say. "That's more like it!"

You hold up a thick marker pen.

"Yes." You look at me, face full of mischief.

"No," I say.

You go back into the drawer and pull out another.

"Leave them, Thor. They're not mine."

"So whose are they?"

"I dunno. Dad's? Diane's?"

You throw one at me and I snatch it out of the air just before it hits my face.

"Thor!"

Another pen comes flying my way. Then another. And another.

You slam the drawer closed and try to open the bottom one. It doesn't budge. You pull harder, shaking the whole cabinet.

"It's locked."

You kick the drawer and the metal bang makes me

look nervously towards the shop. Piano music, but no response from Dad. Maybe he's with a customer.

"Keep it down!" I say.

You tread on the thrown papers as you pick up the pens. "These should be enough for a start."

"A start of what?"

But, watching you staring at the blank walls, I already know your plan.

☆

"A robot's face?" you say.

I punch your arm. *"It's a house! It's your house!"*

"Coral's?"

"Yes! Look, the step, the sticky-out windowsill thing?"

"It looks like a robot's face."

"Yeah, well, maybe if you'd made me with actual hands, I might be a little bit more skilled with a pen."

"I didn't want another writer," you say.

"Clever you. So let's see you do better then. Artsy fartsy."

You step back and survey the wall, tapping the pen against the back of your hand.

"I don't know what to draw," you say.

"*Draw anything. Draw the killer rhino shark.*"

"I'm not nine any more, Thor."

"*So? Draw something that a nearly-eighteen-year-old would draw then. Draw a university.*"

"Funny."

"*I don't know. Who cares? Draw a thought.*"

"Like what?"

"*Anything! Jesus, is this what school does to you? Give me the pen if you're too chicken.*"

I try to grab the pen, but you push me away and pull off the top.

I step back and watch. You stroke the wall, brushing it off like a giant page, then, with one swoop, you make a thick, wet, black line against the grey. The shine of it. I don't know what you're going to draw, but I know it's going to be amazing.

"Knock knock." Your dad is leaning in the doorway. You step back from the wall like you've just been caught by the police. I feel myself grinning.

"Dad, I—"

"I like it," he says, looking at my house. "Robot?"

"It's Coral's house, Karl! Are all your family blind?" He can't hear me. You nod.

"Yeah. Just thought I'd liven up the place a bit. I can paint it over if you want."

"No you can't! Wuss!"

Your dad shakes his head. "No, carry on. I love it. Make it yours. What's this going to be?"

He points at your line. You put the top back on the pen.

"Nothing. Do you need me?"

"Yes, please," he says, "if you've got a second."

"We're busy actually, Karl, if you hadn't noticed. So, if you could just shit off, that'd be great."

Evil eyes.

"Course. Is it the till?"

And you follow him out to the shop.

☆

It takes me a second to register.

He looks tired, in that rock-star kind of way, dark curves under his eyes. His black hair is longer, falling down either side of his face, and he's growing a patchy beard. His dark denim jacket is fashionably battered, over a faded black T-shirt with a distressed collar. He looks like he wants you to think he's in a band.

"Marcie?"

"Hi, Morgan."

I walk to the till, Dad following me like some kind of oversized spirit animal.

"You grew," says Morgan, and I feel his eyes scan me up and down. "Do you work here?"

"Sometimes. Kind of."

Dad leans over my shoulder. "It's her shop."

Morgan looks confused, like he's trying to make the connection between his little sister's best friend and a middle-aged mad scientist.

"This is my dad, Karl. It's his shop."

"You're Karl Baker?" Morgan holds out his hand like he's meeting royalty. "It's a pleasure to meet you, sir."

Dad reaches his hand around me and shakes Morgan's. "No need for the formality. And it's *our* shop."

Morgan nods and lowers his hand. "Cool."

"Well, I'll leave you in Marcie's expert hands. She'll sort out your request."

"Dad. What about running the till? Smacking the day with a banjo?"

"Sorry, Mars –" he taps the top of his head – "had an idea, got to get it down." He starts backing away towards the stairs, shrugging as he goes.

"Good to meet you, sir," says Morgan, almost bowing.

"No sirs here, son," says Dad. Then he's gone.

"This place is pretty cool, eh?" says Morgan, looking around. "How long have you had it?"

There's no way Cara didn't tell him when Dad bought the shop. Testament to an older brother's selective attention.

"Just over three years," I say, neatening up the counter.

Morgan nods like he's viewing a property. "It used to be called something, right? I never came in here before. Nice music."

I move behind the till, trying not to make it obvious that I'm taking him in.

Morgan Miles-Yeung. Former head boy. Two years into a Philosophy degree at UCL.

I swear he was taller.

"*Not this guy.*"

You walk in and lean on the counter next to me, pointing at Morgan. I don't acknowledge you.

"Were you looking for something specific?"

Morgan walks closer.

"I bet he's in a band," you say, mocking. "*Good evening, Glastonbury! We are Poet's Knife!*"

"I ordered two books the other day, over the phone. The lady said they'd be here by today?"

There's a black string necklace against his collarbone.

I pick up the brown package and tear it open. A red-and-white book with black writing slides out.

"*Bird by Bird: Instructions on Writing and Life.*"

"It's not self-help or anything," says Morgan, embarrassed. "I gave my copy to someone and we, well . . . It's really good."

He flashes a smile and I'm twelve in their kitchen, cutting flapjacks with Ken and Cara, while fifteen-year-old him sits on the counter in a Chicago Bulls vest, novel in one hand, glass of milk in the other.

"Are you writing something?" I say.

Morgan shrugs. "Nah, not really."

"Course he is. Look at him. He's probably got Bukowski quotes sharpied up his arm!"

"Shut up." The words slip out. Morgan looks over his shoulder. "Me?"

You start to laugh.

"No, I mean, shut up shop. I have to shut up the shop, for lunch. I'll just take for this. Are you paying with cash?"

"Oh, cash, yeah. Is the other one here too?"

There's no other package.

"I don't think so, sorry. They might have come from different places."

"Oh."

"I could text you when it comes in if you leave your number?"

"*Oh yeah, subtle*."

He starts digging in his pockets. I seize my chance to flash you the middle finger. You put your paws up, pleading innocence.

"Yeah, OK. That'd be great."

He writes his number down on a white bookmark. I ring up the sale.

"Do you want a bag?"

He shakes his head, "Nah, I'm good. Save the trees and whatnot, right?"

Is he nervous? Why would he be nervous?

"*He's not nervous. He's creepy*."

"How's uni?" I say, turning my back on you.

Morgan shrugs. "Yeah. Uni." He pauses. "How'd your exams go?"

"Yeah. Exams." I shrug. "Who knows?"

"*Tell him what you did*."

Grit my teeth. Try to ignore you.

"Cara's so excited about September," I say, a little too loudly. Morgan nods.

"Yep. Stage one of the life plan."

Awkward silence.

"And what about you?" he says.

"What do you mean?"

"I mean, uni, leaving home, chasing your dreams? You up for it?"

"Yeah. It'll be great."

Dodge his eyes.

"What are you studying again?" he says.

"Psychology."

He looks confused. "Not English?"

"What the hell's with all the questions, Morgan?"

"I don't like being told what to read," I say.

Morgan nods, seemingly impressed. "Fair enough. Carve your own path, I guess." He looks round the shelves. "Pretty sweet summer job too."

"Guess so. Dad's not exactly salesman of the year."

Morgan shakes his head. "He's an artist. He doesn't need to be."

You yawn. "*Fartist more like*."

Another silence.

"OK, so you'll text me when it comes, the book?"

I nod.

"Thanks, Marcie. Good to see you."

You pretend to throw up. Morgan leaves.

"Never liked him."

You're sitting on the counter.

"Always thought he was so smart. Ooh, everybody, look at me, super-cool big brother university brainbox Morgan, now I've got a little beard and long hair, whoop di doo."

I lock the door.

"You can't do that, Thor."

"You see him looking at you? Creep."

"I saw you being a dick, that's what I saw."

"Me? I'm not the one buying self-help books, am I?"

"Maybe you should. Maybe you should buy one called *How to Not Be a Dick*."

"Funny. What's he sniffing round you for?"

"He wasn't sniffing round me. He came for a book. You can't say stuff when I'm with people I know. That was a rule."

"Exactly, people you know."

"I know him. He's Morgan."

"You don't know him. Trust me. I've met people like him."

"Yeah? Where?"

"Doesn't matter. He'll be back. Probably write a song about you or some shit."

"Shut up. You did it with Dad too."

"Chill out, yeah?"

My stomach twists in on itself.

"Don't tell me to chill out."

"You always kissed his arse. I love your new trainers, Morgan. Cool T-shirt, Morgan."

"No I didn't."

"Yeah you did. Ooh, he's so cool. I wish I had a big brother like him. He's so fit."

"You haven't got a clue, Thor Baker. Why are you so bothered about Morgan anyway?"

"Sly way to get his number too, by the way. Ring him later. You could go and watch a French film together."

"Enough! Look, I'm going upstairs to see my dad and make a coffee. Either you stop being an idiot or just leave."

You stare at me. I stare back. You jump down off the counter, chest puffed up. You're a full head taller than me.

"You're not the boss of me, Little Marcie. I leave when I want to."

"Yeah?"

Your chest deflates. "No, but come on. I'm just looking out for you."

"Oh yeah? And since when do you do that?"

You step back like I pushed you. I go to the counter.

"I'm not interested in Morgan, Thor. This isn't a YA novel."

I throw the torn packaging into the bin. "I'm not a little girl any more." I stare at you.

"I know," you say.

"Yeah, well, you clearly don't know everything, do you?"

Then you grimace, not offended, more in pain.

"What's wrong?"

You shake your head. You look like you're going to cry. "What is it, Thor?" I walk to you.

"It's just . . ." You look down.

I put my hand on your shoulder. "Hey. It's OK, you can tell me. It's just what?"

You look up and point at my mouth. "It's just . . . you've got spinach in your teeth."

"What?" I pick at my teeth with a nail, then realise I haven't even eaten any spinach.

You're laughing. Paws above your head in triumph.

"So easy!"

I take a deep breath, and punch you in the stomach as hard as I can. You fold in half, wheezing like a punctured air bed.

"That's what you get, Bearboy. Now get lost. Come back when you're not seven."

I watch anger and guilt fight it out in your eyes.

Your mouth opens, and I prepare myself for some barbed-wire comment.

Then you're gone.

☆

Dark landing.

Blurred corridor.

My heart is thumping. Deep breaths.

Look at your bedroom door. Something feels wrong.

Like a part of me is missing.

Like actual atoms from my body aren't here.

I touch my stomach. My chest. My face.

What the hell was that?

☆

"You have to come, Mars!"

We're in the kitchen, eating an extra-large Domino's pizza. My half pepperoni, Cara's half vegetarian. She's two slices behind. The patio door is open. It's nearly eight o'clock. Coral's text said she's stopping at Nick Fury's. Must be going well.

"Can't he advertise or something? I'm sure there's agencies for that."

"This is my dad we're talking about, Car. He's quite particular."

"Peculiar."

"That too. Some stranger wouldn't last five minutes."

I scoop up a couple of pieces of stray sausage and add them to my slice.

Cara groans. "But it'll be so cool! Leia said Jordan's mum's house is literally right on the beach, and we'll have it all to ourselves!"

It does sound good. A week in Cornwall, no parents. Sea. Sun.

"It'll be messy," I say.

Cara nods excitedly. "Yeah! It will."

Picture the gang of them. Bathing suits and bottled beers. Barbeques and beach towels.

Then I picture Dad. Sitting at his table, staring out of the window, surrounded by screwed-up paper. Him behind the till, looking lost, alone in the empty shop.

"I can't, Car." I drop my unfinished slice in the box. "But I want regular updates."

Cara checks her phone.

"Sean will be gutted," she says, trying one last poke at my guilt button. I see her watching him, across a beach fire, faces glowing, drinking and smoking, me fading into the background.

"He'll be fine. He'll have you to keep him company."

I smile, and wait for her to.

When she does, we both know it's case closed.

☆

I walk through the park.

The sun's almost gone and the open green spaces are nearly empty. A few stragglers settling down on their chosen benches. An old couple, sitting defiantly on a chequered blanket, squeezing the last seconds out of a romantic picnic.

Come back when you're not seven.

Yeah, because you're so mature, right, Marcie?

I am what you made me.

My body still feels weird. Like I'm hungry, but don't want to eat.

As I get closer to the middle of the park, the regular rhythm of tabla drumming and choral chants gets louder. The Lost are gathered like always, praying to be found.

The central quadrant with the rocket fountain is squared by a high wall of thick privets with just a door-sized gap on either side. I get a glimpse of the crowd inside as I walk past to the chalky path alongside the hedge. There's the smoky smell and irregular crackle of a fire. I tune my ears and slow my steps, trying to make out their words.

It's not a chant.

What I thought was a group chorus is actually a mess of separate voices all saying different things. All those people, gathered in the same spot, oblivious to the rest of us, maybe even oblivious to each other. I stop walking, put my ear right up to the bush, close my eyes and listen.

Broken pieces of sentences in different voices.

"Do not forget."

"I am not gone."

"Find me."

"I am here."

My brain fits together chunks of unconnected words to make lines of my own, until it feels like the sentences are outside and inside my head at the same time. The low, booming drum travels through me, and I'm swaying, pressed against a privet hedge at dusk.

Then one voice rises above the others. A voice I know, poking up out of the stream of sound.

He's completely naked.

His pale skin almost ghostly in the twilight. His body is lean, but tired, the edges of muscles starting to droop, everything hanging low.

The fire is in the emptied pool of the fountain. Broken branches and belongings. A scruffy orang-utan in a dirty white linen suit with circular mirror sunglasses and a grey beard down to his waist is sitting on the smooth stone edge, palming the drum between his thighs in a trance.

Maybe fifty other people and creatures are standing, sitting, dancing and kicking up dust from the floor, and in the middle of them, three metres in front of me, the only one with no clothes, is Leyland, standing with his eyes closed, arms raised above his head, speaking to no one.

Nobody even acknowledges me as I walk to him.

"Leyland. What are you doing?"

"I cannot steal what is mine. I am you, you are me."

I tap his shoulder. “Leyland.”

He slowly opens his eyes. “Thor Baker.”

He lowers his arms and smiles. “I’m glad you’re here.”

“Where are your clothes?” I say, looking around.

“I burned them.”

“You what? Why?”

Leyland shrugs. “I was hot.”

“Are you high? Come on. I’ll take you home.”

I put my arm around his shoulders, but he slips out and starts to dance. Lifting one foot off the ground, bobbing at the knees.

“Leyland, let’s go. This is weird.”

“So weird!” he shouts. “Weird with a capital woooo!”

He claps his hands and beckons me to dance with him. What looks like a skinny panda dances closer to Leyland, seemingly tuning into whatever energy he’s giving off.

“Leyland. Come on!”

Skinny panda holds out a long paw for Leyland to take. Leyland goes to take it. I grab him before he can and throw him over my shoulder.

*

The funny thing about walking through Fridge City at night with a naked, middle-aged man over your shoulder, mumbling nonsense and laughing, is: nobody even seems to notice.

Welcome to the not real.

I sit him down on the sofa and go to the grand wardrobe in the corner.

"You should lock your door, you know." I grab his dark dressing gown.

Leyland's place is smaller than mine. There's no bedroom; his single bed folds down from the wall next to the door to the tiny kitchen. Bookcases run round the rest of the walls, shrinking the room even more. Piles of different types of paper and card, notebooks and brown box files are arranged in the kind of system that nobody else would understand. The thick desk holds the old-school guillotine, the glue press and balls of twine. The tools of a book-maker. Behind it, the door to the roof has slatted wooden blinds pulled down over the glass. Everything feels collected and full of meaning. Even the three faded brown damp rings on the low ceiling look like the empty puffs of a thought bubble from some ancient comic.

"Come on, help me out, old man."

I ease him into the dressing gown. "Shall I make tea?"

Leyland just stares out. I go into the kitchen and fill the kettle.

"I need some Miles," he says, finally.

I'm in the armchair he usually sits in, across the thick coffee table, sipping my bitter green tea. "Yeah? OK. Which one do you want?"

I go over to the shelf with his turntable and the small stack of vinyl.

"*Kind of Blue*," he says, taking a sip.

I load it up and sit back down.

Warm, sleepy piano crawls out.

How many times have I sat where he's sitting, scored by some old jazz album while I ask him for advice?

A few.

"You look tired, Thor."

"You too," I say.

He reaches for his cigarettes on the coffee table and smiles. “No need to panic, my young friend. I’m still me.”

He taps one out and lights up.

“So what was that then?” I say. “Research?”

Leyland lets out a gentle laugh. “It’s all research, Thor.”

“You don’t belong there, Leyland. With them.”

“No?”

“No. You’re not lost.”

“Not until we are lost do we begin to understand ourselves.” He stares at his lighter. “I’m getting old, Thor.”

“So what? Everybody gets old. I’m getting old.”

“That’s true, but, when you reach the point I have, the getting gets a little quicker.”

He smokes. I sip, wishing I had something profound to say. Something that doesn’t make me want to reach down my own throat and pull my guts out. I don’t.

I think of you. Where you are. What you’re doing.

“I crossed over,” I say, feeling the crackle in my stomach.

Leyland stares at me through the smoke.

"I see."

"That's it? That's all you're gonna say?"

"And what would I say, Thor? That you're making a mistake? That you're dicing with tragedy?"

"I don't know. Something."

Leyland sighs. "You're making a big mistake, Thor. You're dicing with tragedy."

He combs back his hair with his fingers and I guess I should be relieved that he doesn't launch into some sanctimonious lecture, but it's annoying.

"No big deal then," I say, spreading sarcasm over my words. "Sorry I mentioned it."

"My final test was the book," he says, pointing over to his desk.

"What book?" I say. "I don't see a book."

Leyland looks down at his hands like they're an old photograph.

"All I had to do was arrange the pages, set the spine, speak the first line, and I was there. In the real. Seven little words. Double-spaced. Courier font."

"What book, Leyland? What words?"

He mutters something under his breath.

"What did you say?"

He leans forward and flicks his ash in an old saucer on the coffee table.

"I said, *We give ourselves, until the fade. We live for you, we are . . .*"

He waits for me to finish the line from the oath.

". . . *the made.*"

"Thank you. Please collect two hundred as you pass go."

He sits back and takes a deep drag.

"I know how much you want it, Thor. I remember. So badly, it burns. But you have to let it go."

Sitting in your garden. Your face as you took my paw.

"I don't want to, Leyland."

I stare across at him. My elder. Mentor. Tree of wisdom.

Shrinking all the time.

He stares back, and shakes his head.

"Neither did I."

★

You're ten.

It's the middle of the summer holidays.

You're in your pyjamas, standing in the hallway, looking down at the post on the welcome mat.

Coral is in the kitchen, making breakfast.

There's a brown letter that looks like a bill, a glossy flyer for a local hardware company, and a thin white envelope, handwritten address, and your name. You look back down the hall towards the kitchen. Coral is singing along to Sade.

You pick up the envelope and run upstairs.

On your bed you look at the writing. The sloping black letters of your name look more grown-up than they ever have.

The stamp is international and the postmark says Madrid.

You turn it over. It's too flimsy for a card. This is a letter.

Handwritten to you.

You picture her face, smiling as she pirouettes on the dark rug in your old living room, beckoning you to join her. You remember wanting to, but feeling nervous of getting it wrong.

Coral calls you from downstairs.

You pull the old box file from under your bed and take out your brown sketchbook. You pull off the elastic band, open the back cover and slot the envelope inside. You bite your bottom lip, feeling something between confused and excited, then close the book, wrap the elastic band round, lay it in the box and slide it back under your bed.

You shout to Coral that you're coming, then close your eyes, and smile.

☆

"*Psst*. Yo. Wake up."

You look bigger in the dark. Light from my bedroom window gives your chiselled body a halo.

"What time is it?"

"It's late. Early. Who cares?"

I sit up and rub my eyes. Everything is witching-hour quiet.

"What are you doing here, Thor?"

You step forward and light falls on your face. "I'm sorry. For before. In the shop."

Your face twitches as you say it. I fold my arms. "What's the punchline?"

"Shut up." You sit down on my bed and look at me. "I'm sorry, Marcie. I don't know why I did it."

And I can't even laugh.

"Where's Thor Baker?"

"I'm Thor Baker."

"The Thor Baker I know doesn't apologise."

You reach out your paw. "This one does."

The shiny black pad of your palm. I lay my hand on top.

You smile. "Cool?"

I nod.

"All right then. Now get dressed."

Moonlight dusts the grass like icing sugar.

We sit on the outside edge of the bandstand, leaning against the railings, looking back down at the empty park, stretching out either side to the black of the trees. I haven't sat here for years.

"It's not even scary," I say, burrowing my hands into my hoodie pockets.

"Of course not. I'm here."

"It's kind of beautiful."

You let out a sigh. "Yeah. I might write a poem."

You move your leg just before I punch it. Way down at the bottom, past the arts centre, the cricket ground building looks like a giant silver pebble.

I tilt my head back and look up into the bandstand rafters. A monochrome collage of peeling paint and pigeon shit.

"I'm surprised they haven't knocked this down."

"Why would they do that?"

"Because nobody comes here. It doesn't do anything."

"That's a pretty shitty way of looking at things."

"Yeah. Maybe."

Your foot brushes mine. We're older now.

"Ask me a question," you say, staring out.

"About what?"

"Anything."

"I thought that wasn't allowed. What about the rules?"

"Screw the rules." You scratch at the concrete between us with a claw. The air feels charged.

"Could you see me?" I say. "Could you see me this whole time?"

You look at me. "Only when I chose to."

I cross my legs.

"I think I could feel it. When you did."

You cross your legs too.

"I know."

Out of nowhere, a fox appears to our right.

It looks our way for a moment, then cuts across the grass, about six metres in front of us, like a dark knife with legs. We watch it silently scurry all the way to the trees and it feels like we're witnessing something magical.

"You think he had George Clooney's voice?" you say after the fox disappears into the dark.

"What makes you so sure it was a boy?"

There's the faint sound of a breeze passing through leaves.

"My turn," you say.

I squeeze my keys in my pocket. "Go on then."

"Are you sure it's what you want? For them?"

I bring my knees together and wrap my arms around them.

"Yes."

Your dark eyes catch the moonlight.

"So prove it."

And you smile. That first smile I remember. The night you arrived.

"I'll help you."

"Yeah?"

You jump down on to the grass. "Why else am I here?"

Then you spin round and smack my foot.

"Ow! What's that for?"

"Lost time. This is way too grown-up. Let's go scratch something into a tree."

Then you're off, the same way the fox went.

So I follow.

And it feels just as good as I remember.

WEDNESDAY

(7 DAYS LEFT)

The siren of my alarm.

It was somebody's job to design that sound. Somebody so annoying they just channelled their own natural frequency and put it in our phones.

Lance. Lance Finchley. Face like a koi carp, heavy-handed with the Lynx deodorant. The kind of guy who corrects you when you say "borrow" instead of "lend".

Reach out. Off. "Shut up, Lance."

"Marcie?"

A muffled voice.

"Marcie?"

It's Cara, speaking from under my duvet. Wasn't my alarm, it was an incoming call.

"Hello?"

"Were you sleeping?"

Everything feels too bright. My eyes sting.

"Are you even dressed?"

I look down at myself. I'm still in my clothes. It was almost light when we got back. Passed out. Didn't even take my shoes off. I can smell outside on my hoodie.

"Yes. I'm dressed. What time is it?"

"It's nearly eleven."

"Shit."

"Aren't you supposed to be at the shop?"

"Yeah. Overslept. Stayed up late."

"Doing what?"

Your smile as you peeled away bark with your claws. Carving our initials.

"Nothing. YouTube wormhole. Started on a Kendrick Lamar video, ended up on some Illuminati documentary."

"Nice. You wanna meet later? I'm leaving tomorrow."

"Oh yeah, the beach. Yeah, what shall we do?"

"Cinema? Or I could come over?"

I sit up and rub my eyes.

"Cinema sounds good. What's on?"

"Who cares? Come to mine when you finish at the shop, OK? I'll buy the popcorn."

"OK. See you later."

"Oh, and, Mars?"

"Yeah?"

"Who's Sean's favourite rapper?"

It looks like a garage sale.

Bits of equipment and bric-a-brac are spread out over every surface of the living room.

A couple of outdated laptops. A sewing machine. Shoes. A dusty white lamp projector. Little towers of stacked books. Bin bags of clothes. Dad is on his knees, fiddling with the underside of his old electronic typewriter.

"What are you doing?" I say.

Dad looks up at me, then round at the mess of the room. His hair is even more out of control than usual, sticking up in all directions like a jagged comic-book explosion.

"I found it," he says, patting the navy-blue plastic body. "It took me all night, but I found it."

"The typewriter?"

"Exactly! THE typewriter. My trusty steed. None of this spellcheck, software update crap. Just a green screen. Black font. No excuses. If I can just get it working . . ." He digs into the battery cavity with a finger. "How's the shop?"

"I just got here, Dad."

"Cool. What time is it?"

"It's nearly twelve."

"Splendid. There's coffee in the pot."

He looks like one of those people from the Channel Five programmes about hoarders. Some middle-aged guy who hasn't thrown anything away for twenty-five years.

"Are you OK, Dad?"

"I need power."

"What?"

"Batteries, Mars." He stands up and puts the lifeless typewriter down on the table. I read the word "brother" in a stylised font next to the thin display screen. If I had a Sharpie, I could prefix it with "little".

"Does any of this stuff still work?"

"I have no idea. Be fun to smash up if it doesn't."

"But you're OK though?"

He walks over and hugs me. "I'm fine, Mars. Lots to do."

He lets go and smiles the kind of smile that could charm a lump of concrete.

"Don't worry about your old man. Unhinged works for him."

"And what about his daughter?" I say. "Is she half unhinged?"

"I'm afraid so." He nods gravely, then grins. "Luckily for her, she's half something else too. That's why she's the hero of the piece."

£21.97

That's what I've taken for the till in nearly four hours.

Roughly £5.50 an hour.

I'm no Alan Sugar but I'm pretty sure that's not great turnover.

I look up at the ceiling and try to imagine a conversation about money with Dad. The painful comedy sketch of the pair of us attempting to outline a business plan.

I have a memory of going to the birthday party of two twin blonde girls in the Infants. I don't remember their names. I do remember turning up to their house without a gift because Dad forgot, and I do remember him taking out a twenty-pound note, tearing it in half, handing a half to each girl, saying, "Ten for you, and ten for you." The look on their faces. On their mum's face.

I open Google on my phone and type in "average university student debt".

. . . a typical student on a three-year course outside London might expect to graduate with around £35,000–£40,000 of student loans . . .

I look across at the nearest display table and make the books stacks of banded notes like in *Breaking Bad*. How big a pile would £40,000 be?

I know that it's not like you graduate and then there's these two massive loan-shark guys waiting by the door with baseball bats, saying give us our forty g's or we kneecap you. I know you only start paying it back when you're earning a certain amount and then it's just a bit every month, but a debt is a debt, right? Doing something that puts you in somebody else's pocket is bad practice, no?

Like I even think like that.

Like money is anything more than an idea to me, floating around, like religion or politics or rising sea levels. I know what they mean. I know they matter. But saying that I think about them on a daily basis would be a lie. Never had loads of money, never had none.

Forty thousand. Fifty thousand. May as well be two million. It's just some abstract number that people will bring up when trying to convince themselves that doing a degree is a bad idea.

Truth is, no matter how unfair it is, if you really want to go, you're going, massive debt or not.

All that stuff can be worried about later. Right now, nobody is thinking past getting the grades, and knowing that they didn't mess up. That's the truth of it.

I sound like you.

Where are you right now? Passed out on your bed, wherever that is?

Are you coming? Are you watching?

I type "university clearing" into Google.

Then Sean walks in.

His head is freshly shaved.

Black T-shirt, faded black jeans, battered black Vans. He's holding a hemp shopping bag.

You won't come if Sean's here. I know that.

"Is it smaller?" he says, looking round.

"Yeah, Sean. We shrunk it last year. I'm trying to make people think they're going crazy. It's like *The Twits*."

"All right, I'm just saying. I guess we grew."

"What do you want?"

"What, can't you read my mind, Miss Psychologist?"

He waves his hands around his head.

"That's not what psychology is, you idiot. I'm not Derren Brown."

"Mind control?" he says, hopefully.

I shake my head. "Afraid not. Whose birthday is it?" I say.

"No one's. Maybe I'm here to buy a book for me."

"You don't read, Sean."

"Yeah I do! Sometimes. What's this?"

He cocks his head, trying to work out what the music is.

"DJ Shadow. You have the album."

"Don't think so."

"I copied it for you in Year Nine."

Sean shrugs. "Lots happened since then. Here."

He walks over to me and puts three graphic novels on the counter. It's the first three volumes of Scott Snyder and Greg Capullo's *New 52* series for DC. I smile.

"You've already read them, haven't you?" Sean says, disappointed.

"Yeah. It's really good. There's more too, if you like them?"

"Should've known. Some things don't change, eh?"

"Nope."

"So you're not coming, to the seaside?"

I have to laugh.

"What?"

"I don't think you're allowed to call it 'the seaside' any more."

He laughs. "That's what it is! The seaside. What else am I gonna call it? The beach? That sounds like I think we live in California or something. Seaside still feels right to me."

"Maybe that's because you're still seven."

"Maybe I am. So stop trying to kill my magical seven-year-old outlook on the world, Mrs Mature."

"That sounds like a brand of cheese."

"Well, truth hurts, Mars."

I throw my pen at him. He catches it and slides it into his pocket.

"How's your old man?"

I look back to the doorway. Johnny Cash winks at me from the shelf.

"Still Dad."

"Is he writing?"

"Always."

We both look back at the stairs for enough time to change the subject.

"It suits you," he says, making a camera frame with his fingers. "Bookshop hero."

"Shut up."

"I'm serious. I'd trust your recommendations. I mean, if I read books."

"You should try it some time."

He picks up a grey novel from the corner of the display table. "Remember when you used to read to me?"

Hooks in my heart.

"Course."

"What was that one, with the angel guy, in the shed?"

"*Skellig*."

"Yeah. I liked that one. When was that?"

"Year Five. Miss Secker's class."

"Secker! Witch! Remember she used to make me read out loud? Said I was lazy."

"You were lazy, Sean."

"Yeah, but that wasn't why I was no good at reading. Racist."

And we both laugh. Me and Sean Johnson. Kano

lookalike. Lion-hearted idiot. Loyal enough to cover for me, through all that pain.

"I'll miss this," he says.

"What?"

"When you're gone. I'll miss hanging out."

"We don't hang out."

"No, I know, not like before, but, I mean, we could've. When you're gone though, you're, well, gone, eh?"

He looks right at me like a lost puppy, and it is sad how things changed, but how could they not?

"How's your nan?" I say.

"She's all right. Still worrying. She misses you."

"I miss her. I get a craving for her stewed chicken at least once a day."

We both smile. Leona's cooking is next level.

"She must be happy you finished A-levels though?"

"Yeah, but she wanted me to go to uni."

"You still can. If you want."

"I don't think so, Mars. School and me are done. Over. I'm filing for divorce."

"I'm sorry to hear that."

"Yeah. And she gets to keep the house."

"And what do you get?"

"I dunno. Freedom?"

"Sounds good."

Sean rolls his eyes, "Yeah. Filing documents in some accountant's office for one of Nan's church friends. World-changing stuff."

"Don't say that. A job is good."

"No, doing nothing is good. A job is a ball ache." He puts the book back. "It'll mean I can give her a bit each week though. Help out."

"Exactly, and you'll have some cash for equipment and stuff too, right?"

"I guess. Could do with a decent mic."

"See? Funding your art. That's how it starts. You'll write your best stuff on the back of tax-return printouts."

Sean nods along, enjoying the idea.

"And what about your art, Mars? You just gonna stop?"

I think of the wall in the back room. The black pen. And I shrug.

"But you're so good!" Sean says. "Why not an art degree? Or foundation or whatever they call it, instead of brain science?"

"I need to lock up," I say.

"The offer for EP cover art is still there, you know? If

you change your mind? We've got a bit of cash to pay you."

"I don't think so."

I power down the till, and for a second I swear I see you in the corner.

"Come with us, Mars! It'll be fun. You can draw on the beach. Your dad can watch the shop for a week, can't he?"

"Leave it, Sean."

He's not giving up though. "Can I go say hello? I haven't seen him in ages."

He starts to head for the door. I come out from behind the counter and block his path.

You're not here but I can feel you. Watching.

"He's working. Better not."

"Just a quick hello."

"He's in his little bubble, Sean. The only way he'll get anything done is if there's no other distractions, like running a shop."

His shoulders slump, defeated. "OK."

Your eyes, on me.

"I do need a favour though." I say.

"Course. Anything. What is it?"

"Cara."

Can you see, Thor?

"What do you mean?" says Sean.

"I just think . . . doesn't matter."

"What is it, Mars?"

The crackle in my stomach.

"She'd kill me if she knew I said anything to you."

"About what?"

He's genuinely oblivious.

I know you can see me.

"Marcie, what about Cara?"

Watch me, Thor.

I look right at Sean.

"She likes Jordan."

☆

You're not quite in the back row but near enough.

Cara is sitting to your right, the popcorn jammed in the armrest between you. Ryan Gosling is on the toilet, sitting in a cubicle with his arm in a cast. Russell Crowe is banging on the door. The film isn't very good, but Cara's eyes are glued to the screen.

Her fingers reach for more popcorn and miss the tub, brushing your hand. She looks at you. You smile. She takes some popcorn and goes back to the film. You lean back in your seat and touch the back of your hand where her fingers were.

☆

I pull the page out of the typewriter and add it to the rest.

My claws stroke the old box file as I stare out of the window at the dark violet sky.

I saw what you did, Marcie, in the shop.

Just like you wanted.

Just like you said.

THURSDAY

(6 DAYS LEFT)

THOR BAKER:
FADE COUNSELLING SESSION 4

8AM

I'm not in denial.

If you say so.

I'm just saying, there's no point moping around, right?

I suppose not. So long as you remember what's happening.

Like I could forget?

Have you experienced any physical sensations?

Like what?

Like fatigue? Or an emptiness? Blurred vision?

I don't know.

Which one?

All of them.

I see.

Is that normal?

Yes. How do you feel now?

I feel OK. Is that wrong?

No. You just need to keep hold of the situation. You'll feel these things as you get closer to the fade. Time is ticking down, Thor.

I know.

So it's going well, with her?

Yeah.

That's good. Important to enjoy the time you have left.

I'm helping. I mean, I feel like I'm helping. We talked. It was good.

That's great. What did you talk about?

Just stuff.

What kind of stuff?

Just, you know, stuff. I'm not going to go into details, Alan. It's private.

You haven't spoken about here, have you?

Our sessions?

The not real. You haven't told her anything about this side?

No.

Good. You know how important that is.

Quite convenient though, isn't it? That she can't know. That she's completely oblivious to all this. To here.

The rules are there for a good reason.

I know, I know. Not like it matters anyway. The fade's the fade, right?

It matters, Thor. Trust me.

OK.

So I have your word?

Whatever.

I'm serious.

Yeah. And I'm late.

☆

The sound of tap-dancing fingertips.

Dad's actually typing.

He's in just his vest and pants and his hair looks like the vertical trail of a meteorite. There's an untouched coffee next to him and the ashtray isn't even half full, which has to be a good sign.

I remember peeking into his room when I was little, seeing him hunched over, the whirring click-clack music of his story machine. Wanting to ask him things, knowing not to interrupt.

I start to tiptoe to the kitchen.

"Morning, Mars," he says, not looking up.

"Morning. How's it going?"

He shrugs, still typing. "I have absolutely no idea."

"OK."

He flashes a grin. "And it feels great."

A wired, mad-scientist smile, and then he's back to it, the letter-filled paper feeding up as he goes.

"I'm not sure, Thor."

"Yes you are."

"It's stupid."

"Says who?"

"Says me."

"So why are we here then?"

"I don't know."

"Yes you do. Don't chicken out now. It's easy – you saw the YouTube video. I'll help."

"I'm scared."

"You're not scared, you're excited."

"I feel scared."

"That's because you can't have excitement without fear. They're part of the same thing. Like Two-Face."

"That's not what Two-Face is about at all. Harvey Dent was all about law and order, then he lost his mind and became obsessed with the arbitrary nature of chance. He's—"

"Shut up! We're doing it. Man, you think too much. Grab both bottles. It's a good job I'm here."

It's blue.

Not the same gas-flame blue as the picture on the packet, but it's blue.

My roots are lighter from the first bleach, then, after a couple of centimetres, the dirty blonde goes almost white before shifting into a deep Gatorade blue.

My scalp is tingling, and my hair looks like a technicolour latte.

We're squished into the tiny downstairs bathroom by the back door of the shop. Your cropped hair came out darker than mine. Just a hint of turquoise. The A4 mirrored door of the medicine cabinet looks like the cover of a magazine. Me and you. Some kind of avant-garde musical duo.

I gently press the side. "It looks like a crap firework."

You bump my shoulder. "It's wicked!"

"It's a clown wig, Thor. Yours looks good – I look like I'm wearing a peacock!"

You laugh, because it's funny.

I laugh, because I'm an idiot.

"What did we do?"

"Relax. It looks cool, plus it'll wash out eventually, right?"

"I don't know. I've never done this before."

"Exactly. New ground. You're a pioneer!"

"Of my own head?"

"Best kind."

Your reflection smiles over my shoulder. I'm fighting it but it does feel good.

Stupid and selfish and good.

There's something about owning a mistake, claiming it as yours, that makes you feel like you've changed.

Like you've learned something about yourself. Something that lets you realise that you get to choose whether it was actually a mistake at all.

Right?

"Exactly."

I feel like I'm on stage.

Sitting behind the counter, waiting for an audience.

A pudgy woman in a polka-dot raincoat comes in just after lunch.

Straight away I know she's not going to buy anything. She does that annoying thing of indiscriminately browsing every single shelf with a completely fake conviction, then asks me if we have a book she already knows isn't there.

When I tell her I can order it, she looks at my hair and does the disappointed tut. "I'll go to the Foyles in town," she says, like I've failed some kind of test.

"*Yeah. Go to Foyles, fatso!*"

I shake my head. You ignore me and get right up close to her. "*They've got a cafe there too, full of food. For your belly!*"

I manage to half disguise my laugh with a cough. The woman turns her nose up and walks out. You follow her to the door, pointing through the glass when it closes. "Blimp."

"That wasn't fair," I say, neatening the non-fiction table.

"She was annoying."

"She was a customer, Thor. We need those."

"She looked like a beach ball."

"Don't be mean. If she's an arse, it's got nothing to do with her weight."

"Why so touchy?"

I sit back down behind the till. "I'm not exactly a size six myself."

"Shut up. You look amazing."

Awkward pause.

We both look down like we dropped something.

"I mean, you look good. That's all I meant."

"Stop talking, Thor."

"Sorry."

Mid-afternoon, a guy who looks about the same age as Diane, dressed like a teacher, comes in looking for Roy Keane's autobiography. Somehow we have it.

"It's for my dad," he says, as he pays. "Last-minute birthday gift."

As I wrap it for him, I watch him consider my hair, mull over a possible compliment, then decide not to comment.

"I always mean to come in here, but never do," he says, apologetically. "Didn't you used to have a name?"

"Blue Pelican Books."

"That's it! So what are you called now?"

"Well, we're still in discussions. But we're here! So, now you've been, come again. And tell your friends."

"I will," he says, nodding as he leaves.

"Tell your friends?"

You're at the fiction shelves.

"What? I'm drumming up business."

"Bit desperate though, eh?"

"Do you see a queue?"

"Fair enough. This place is dry. We should do something to make it less dry."

"Like what?"

"I dunno, do I? You're the one with the imagination."

You wink and point at me like a game-show host.

"Funny."

"Let's go show your dad, see his face."

I sit on the stool and check my phone. "He's working, Thor."

No messages yet.

"They'll be there by now," I say, picturing Cara, Sean and the others giggling as they unpack the car like models on a catalogue photo shoot.

You glare at my phone.

"What?"

"Nothing. Do you reckon I could stack a pile of books taller than me?"

"Why?"

"Bet I can."

"Doubt it."

"Bet me then."

"Bet you what?"

Your evil mastermind grin.

"I like it," says Dad, nodding like a scientist reviewing test results.

"Yeah?"

"Yeah. Makes me want a cocktail. Marcie Colada." He chuckles to himself. "Wish I could be there when Coral sees it."

"Why don't you come for dinner? She'd be happy to see you."

Dad looks back at the table. There's a small pile of

typed pages on one side of the typewriter, a stack of blank paper on the other. "Not tonight, Mars. I'm right in it. The eye of the storm. Don't want to break my rhythm."

"Course not. Soon though? You haven't been over in ages."

"Yeah. Soon."

He squeezes my shoulder, oblivious to you on the sofa, grinning the whole time.

Cara: **This place is gorgeous! Wish u were here, Mars xx**

Me: **Have fun for me. Daily updates required ;) x**

Cara: **Affirmative. Beach party tonight. Fingers crossed x**

The pang of guilt.

The crackle of trouble.

I am seventeen.

I am seven.

"Holy shit!"

Coral stands in the living-room doorway, covering her mouth, like she's wary of what else might jump out. I press pause on *Mario Kart*.

"I'm sorry," she says, through her fingers. "It's just . . . it's blue."

"Yep."

"Wow. I mean, wow, Mars. What brought this on?"

"Dunno. I always wanted to try it."

"You did?"

"Yeah."

"I see." She puts her handbag down on the dresser and walks over.

"Did you go to a salon?" she says, touching the side of my hair like it's a newly discovered material.

"Nope. Did it myself."

"Wow. OK. Good for you."

"You hate it."

"No! I mean, it's pretty, I don't know, loud, but it kind of suits you." She leans back to take me in, like a sculpture. "Who'd have thought?"

"I would."

You're sitting on the floor in front of the TV.

I shrug. Coral points at the flashing neon squares of the Rainbow Road track. "Been a while since you played computer games, hasn't it?"

"Just felt like it."

"OK, well, I guess you've earned some down time, right? Listen, I've invited Dom for dinner on Saturday night. I thought it'd be a chance for you to get to know each other a bit better."

"OK."

You roll your eyes. "*Boring.*"

"All right, good. Well, I have marking to do, so . . ." She starts to leave.

"Is he a professor then?" I say.

Coral smiles. "A doctor. Of cognitive science. He's head of the department."

"*Sleeping with your boss. Go, Coral.*"

I keep a straight face. "Pretty smart then?"

"Yes. He's a brilliant man. You'll have lots to talk about. He studied at Leeds too."

"*You studied his leeds.*"

"That doesn't make any sense."

"Why not?" asks Coral.

You're laughing.

"No, I mean, no way, I don't believe it. Small world."

Coral steps closer and inspects my eyes.

"What are you doing?" I say.

"Just checking. I know you've been with your dad a lot." She mimes smoking a joint.

"I don't smoke, Coral."

"No –" older sister glare – "and neither does your dad."

I lean back on the sofa. "So is he your boyfriend then?"

"Very funny."

She tries to act unfazed, but starts squirming towards the door. "Will you sort dinner, please? I don't have time."

You're smiling, enjoying the role-reversal embarrassment show.

"Yeah. Just let me finish this level."

I unpause the game. Coral breathes out, and leaves the room.

"Great. A chit-chat dinner with Nick Fury. What a waste of a Saturday night that'll be."

I power-slide the last corner and overtake Princess Peach.

"Don't be like that. She likes him. I can tell."

I blast Bowser with my red shell and nick first place.

"Yes!"

We both watch Yoshi's race highlights.

"Who doesn't like Nick Fury?"

"I dunno. Hydra?"

I've won the gold.

"Still got it," I say, shutting down the Wii U. "Some things last forever."

Your shoulders slump. I lightly kick your back. "You gonna help me cook?"

You stay on the floor.

"Thor?"

"You're nearly eighteen." Your voice is solemn.

"So are you."

"Eighteen."

"Nuts, right?"

"Ten years since that night."

"Yeah. What's wrong?"

"Nothing."

"So I can drink legally. Who cares? It's all hype. No big deal."

You nod.

"Yeah. No big deal."

☆

You're nine.

Sitting back left, you watch an awkward, skinny boy with skin the same colour as your dad introduce himself to the class. He's just moved from Bradford to live with his grandma.

His name is Sean.

You recognise an angry sadness in his eyes.

As he speaks, you begin to feel something. A connection.

Other people are only half listening, waiting for break time.

When you look forward again, the boy's eyes are on you.

The teacher tells him to sit down.

He half smiles at you.

You half smile back and make a promise to yourself to find him at break time. You already know you will be friends.

☆

The orange glow of the city fades up into the night sky.

The blinking red dot of a plane slides left through the darkness, pretending to be a shooting star.

Leyland's got his armchair out on the roof and sits reading, a lit cigarette between his fingers.

I take a crate from near his door and sit down next to him.

I think about sitting with you as you'd draw. Watching your eyes move as your pencil sketched a face, a body, a world. I'd sit happily, in a kind of calm trance, all afternoon, as you filled page after page.

No big deal.

"Are you waiting for a thank-you?" says Leyland, not looking up.

"No. I just came to check how you're doing."

Leyland folds the corner of his page and closes the book. The title says *The Stranger*.

"No you didn't."

He crosses one leg over the other and smokes, waiting. There are pebbles and a few crumbs of loose mortar near my feet. I scrape them together into a little mound of miniature rubble.

"We made fajitas," I say, "For her and her aunt."

"Nice."

"I poured hot pepper sauce into the pan when she wasn't looking."

I arrange a little line of stones, smallest to biggest.

"I see."

"The whole bottle."

"Ouch. Spicy."

"They drank a litre of milk between them."

Leyland looks at me. "And you felt bad?"

"No," I say, "not at all."

"OK."

"I never feel bad there. Only now. Only here."

I flick the first pebble. It skips across the tarred floor and hits the low wall. "I can't help it, Leyland. I get there, with her, and I just want trouble."

Leyland grinds his cigarette butt under his heel and lights another.

"We are but what we were made for," he says, brushing ash from his pinstriped trouser leg.

I flick the next pebble along. "It's like there's one me here, and then another me there."

"I know, my friend," he says, leaning back.

"But which one is the real me, Leyland?"

Leyland smiles.

"I'm afraid that's a question only you can answer."

FRIDAY

(5 DAYS LEFT)

Feels like I'm sitting in a dusty photograph.

We never spent much time in this room.

The back room had the TV in it, the stereo and the sofa.

This room always felt too neat, a little front-room museum where you weren't supposed to touch anything.

The dark dresser doesn't have those stupid plates on it any more. China reserved for special guests who never arrived. The pictures have gone from the walls too, leaving rectangles of unfaded wallpaper, and the old gas fireplace looks like it would fall off if you coughed.

I feel heavy today.

What I know is pinning down what I want, pressing it into my chest, squeezing my lungs.

Truth hurts. They say that.

You're lying to yourself, because the truth hurts.

But what about a good truth? What about true comfort, or true laughter, does that hurt?

I know what I'm doing is stupid, but I know it feels good. I know it can't end well, but I know that you want me there. So what's true?

Any of it? All of it?

No big deal.

"Memory lane?"

I'm on my feet in a blink, staring at Blue in the doorway, hands in her pockets, hood pulled up, silver flask under her arm.

The lead weight of guilt sinks in my stomach.

"What are you doing here?"

"Delicate work, eh?" She nods, scanning the untouched room.

"Blue . . ."

"Save it, Thor. It doesn't matter."

"I'm just . . . taking my time."

"I can see."

"You shouldn't be here."

"I didn't come here to fight, OK?" She holds up the flask. "Coffee?"

We sit in the empty kitchen.

I sip from an old beetroot jar that was left on the side. Blue drinks from her flask lid. The coffee is strong and thick. Some kind of bird is singing outside.

"Nice hair," she says. And I want to hide.

"How did you find me?"

"I followed you."

"On the train?"

She shakes her head and points up.

"I thought you didn't fly any more?" I say, blowing on my coffee.

"Yeah, and I thought you were knocking this place down."

"I am. I've put the wall braces in. I've done the roof."

"Half of the roof. It's been nearly a week, Thor."

"I know. I'm taking my time. Getting it right."

"Course."

"It's complicated, Blue."

"I don't doubt it," she says, sipping slowly.

"I am going to knock it down. I know I have to."

She doesn't respond. I swig a mouthful and wince as it burns my throat.

"I've still got a few days."

"And then what? You'll just calmly knock it all down and get on with your life?"

"I thought you didn't come to fight?"

I roll the jar between my paws. My brain feels fuzzy.

"She's messing with your head, Thor. She's not even here and she's messing with you."

"It's not that simple."

"You got that right."

She finishes her coffee and pours herself another.

"Blue, look, there are things you don't understand. It was different for you, you weren't sent away. It's more blurred; the lines, they—"

"You crossed over, didn't you?"

"What?"

"Didn't you?"

She's leaning forward in her seat, staring, her blonde hair almost glowing in the half-light.

"Blue, look . . ."

"You idiot."

"No, listen . . ."

"You stupid, stupid boy."

I lean back in my chair, her eyes burning a hole in my chest.

"She needs me," I say.

Blue's sigh almost fills the room. She closes her eyes, shaking her head. "They all need us, Thor. Until they don't. Until they forget. Or throw us away."

"She didn't throw me away." My paws push down on the veneered table.

"Yes she did. Like a bag of rubbish."

The muscles in my arms twist and tighten. I can feel prickles in my chest. "Leave it, Blue, please."

"And what? Just stand by and watch you drive yourself mad? I'm worried about you, Thor. You can't fight the fade."

"I'm not going mad, OK? I'm in control."

She laughs. "You almost sounded like you actually believe that."

"I do. I decide. When I cross. If I cross. It's up to me."

"Are you listening to yourself?"

"It's true! The door. I *choose*."

"What door?"

"My final test. It's up to me. I—"

But then I feel it. In the pit of my stomach first, then climbing up my spine, spreading along each rib, like a light, filling me. How? This can't be happening. Blue's staring at me. The heat and the rush. I lift my paws, my coffee jar falls, bounces and dark coffee splashes on the white linoleum floor. "Blue. I didn't. I don't . . ." I reach out to her, but, before she can say anything, I'm in your bedroom, standing by the window. You're sitting on your bed, a look of panic on your face.

☆

"I have to go back."

You're in front of my window, your arms reaching out, confused.

"What?"

"I have to go back. This wasn't . . . I'm not supposed . . . It's not . . . Blue."

"What's not blue? Go back where?"

You stop yourself saying more.

Your eyes close and your arms go down.

"Nowhere. Doesn't matter."

Behind you the sky is wet newspaper grey.

"Are you OK, Thor?"

"I'm fine. What happened?"

"I had the dream."

"What dream?"

"The same one. About what happened. To Sean."

You look down at your hands. "I should go, Marcie."

Shake my head. "Please stay."

You lie down next to me. The two of us on my bed. Like before. When it was easy.

Some kind of bird is singing outside.

"I remember that crack," you say, pointing at the black cardiograph line in the ceiling. "I saw it that first night."

"I think it grew," I say, my forearm brushing the rough fur of yours. "Do you think that means the house is slowly coming down?"

"Yeah. Slowly."

I breathe in and wait, breathing out in sync when you exhale.

You're thinking something loud. Something you want to say but can't.

"What did I do, Thor? What have I done?"

I turn my head. You stare up at the crack.

"Exactly what you wanted to."

Birmingham monsoon.

The kind of fat raindrops that splash on your tongue.

Dark thunderclouds smother the sun.

I keep my hair under the umbrella. You happily stomp through puddles ahead of me like you're following a giant's footsteps.

"Why so happy?" I say.

You look back over your shoulder, a big grin on your face. "Purpose." You do a high two-footed jump and splash into a deep puddle at the base of a tree.

"Remember when it used to rain and then after you'd make me come with you on 'operation snail rescue'?"

"Course I do."

"We must've saved hundreds."

"Yep. And nobody even knew."

You strike a karate pose. "Invisible heroes!"

I stop walking. "What do you do, Thor? When you're not with me?"

You turn on your heels, still in attack stance, the fur on your arms dark and drenched.

"I smash stuff."

Heavy droplets thump against the umbrella skin. "That's all I'm getting?"

"'Fraid so."

"This isn't normal though, is it?"

You spread your arms and walk backwards. I step back from the kerb as a bus approaches. You see it coming and stand fast.

"What the hell's normal?"

And you smile as a tidal wave of gutter water hits you in the chest.

Bliss

noun

1. Supreme happiness; utter joy or contentment: the feeling of being left alone in a room full of books on

a rainy day with a good coffee and no adults giving you grief.

– *Dictionary of Marcie,* **Oxford Press**

It's like the best wet break ever.

Dad's writing upstairs. The shop is empty. *Ella and Louis* on the stereo. You're in the corner by the window. I sit behind the till, feeling the calm of time slowing down.

"Let's move stuff around," you say.

"What do you mean?"

You're already pushing the display tables together, easing them both to the back of the room.

"Thor, what are you doing, what about customers?"

"What customers?" And you walk out the back.

"Hey!"

The front of the shop looks bigger with the space. I hear a sharp squeaking sound, then you come through, dragging the old brown sofa from the back room with you.

"What's that for?"

"Your arse."

You push it into the space where the tables were, leaving

a channel between the back of it and the shelves, then sit down.

"Perfect."

It looks like you're in a living room. One with loads of books.

"Come try it."

I slump down next to you. Sitting this low makes everything feel more open. Higher.

"See?"

I nod.

"People can sit here and read. Get cosy."

I point at the displaced display tables. "What about those?"

"Who cares? Put the books somewhere else, find space. You could use one of the tables for biscuits."

"Biscuits?"

"Yeah. And coffee. One of those big silver thermos things."

"Are you talking about a cafe?"

"No. That's long. Just coffee and a biscuit. Make it feel more homely."

"We're a shop, yeah? Not an old people's home."

You stand up. "You mean NO people's home?"

Then something crashes upstairs.

We both look up.

Thumping steps. Another bang. And a tortured scream.

He's on his knees.

Hands in his lap. Surrounded by strewn pages.

The table is on its side, thin legs pointing at him like wooden antennae. The blue typewriter is belly up, next to a dark brown puddle of coffee and his empty mug.

"Dad?"

Typed words, diagrams, frantically scrawled sentences, everywhere. They look like black insects, crawling on the blanket of white paper. The desperate work of a man trying to get ideas down before they fly away.

"Dad?"

I kneel down next to him. "Dad, what happened?"

He closes his eyes and lets out a low groan.

I put my hand on his shoulder. "Hey. It's OK. It's all right."

"No, Mars," he says, "it's all shit."

I look at you, watching from the doorway, and you don't need me to tell you. You just disappear.

THOR BAKER:
(UNSCHEDULED)
FADE COUNSELLING SESSION 5

10.30AM

What happened?

You tell me.

I wasn't expecting you today. Did you dye your hair?

What? Oh, forget that.

You seem flustered.

Do I? That's weird. I mean, it's not like I was called or anything?

You were called?

Yes, Alan. I was called, which seems kind of strange to me, what with all this about my "final test" and everything. Not much of a "final test" if it's not me who decides, is it?

And you're sure?

Like it's something I could be unsure about? It's one thing to hear your name and choose to cross over, but to be actually called, what the hell?

How did it happen?

What do you mean? Same way it always did! I felt it, and then I was there.

I mean, where were you?

Why does that matter? How is it even possible, Alan? What about the door?

Were you in the house?

Yes. In the kitchen.

There you go.

There I go what?

It's the house. If you're in the house, she can call you. That's why you have to knock it down.

Are you serious?

Very. The places where we were made hold power over us, whenever we go back to them. In that house, your maker is in control. This is part of it.

The test?

Yes. You felt it, right? The feeling of the call? How amazing it is?

Yeah.

Which is why you have to get to work, before it's too late.

So, when I destroy the house, I can't be called?

I know it's a lot to take in, Thor, but it's all about choice.

I don't see how. Man, this is so messed up.

That's why I'm here. To help.

What if I can't do it?

You can. And you will.

But how do you know?

Because you have to.

☆

"There."

I add the last of the pages to the pile, using the jagged glass ashtray as a paperweight.

Dad sits on the sofa, staring at the old equipment stacked in front of the fireplace.

The coffee stain on the carpet looks like a nursery-school paw print.

"We might need a skip for all that," I say. "Does any of it even still work?"

Nothing.

"Shall I order one, a skip? Dad?"

"I'm sorry, Mars."

"For what?"

"I know I'm hard work."

He reaches for his tobacco on the coffee table.

I stroke the smooth keys of his typewriter. "Yeah, well. Who wants easy?"

He smiles at me.

"She told me I'd never do it."

"Who did, Diane?"

"Your mum. *You'll die before you finish that book*. That was the last thing she said to me."

My mouth won't work. This is the first new thing he's told me about her since I can remember. I sit down at the table and watch him think of her as he rolls his cigarette.

"She always had a knack of telling me exactly what I needed to hear."

He sparks up and we just sit, the pair of us, filling with different memories.

Flamenco music. Stomping feet. Empty bottles. Screaming through walls. Tears. Silence. Peeking into the living room when it was over. An abandoned crime scene. Tipped furniture and thrown books, pages spread, like dead birds, on the floor.

"I can't see her," I say. "Her face, I mean. I remember things, feelings, but I don't see a face."

Dad blows smoke.

"She had a good face. A great face. But man, she could be cruel."

The rain has stopped, but the street is shiny and soaked.

I touch the typewriter keys to spell out her name.

Each letter feels charged with electricity.

I touch the full stop and look at him. "She wrote me a letter."

Dad's face drops. His hand shakes as he takes the cigarette out of his mouth.

"When?"

"Years ago. It was in the summer holidays, before Year Seven."

Dad looks away.

"I see."

"Madrid 28070. That's what the postmark said. I never told you. I don't know why."

Dad doesn't say anything.

"It's an area code. I googled it."

Dad still doesn't speak.

"Dad. It might be where she lives. The place . . ."

He looks at me, finally, and shakes his head. "I doubt it."

He wants to ask what she said. I can see it in his eyes, a flicker of curiosity. Of jealousy.

The father in him fighting with the jilted man.

"She could be anywhere, Mars."

I see the letter. On the doormat. In my hand. Tearing it open that night. Not knowing what to expect, but expecting something. Anything. The disappointment of seeing one solitary line.

Seven words.

Remember, Marcie. Whatever happens, just be you.

One sentence. Secretly sent by a stranger.

The other half of what I am.

"But it's not impossible, right? There's a chance she's still there?"

Then, like someone flicked a switch at the back of his head, I watch him shut down. His face goes blank, and the invisible wall he built to deal with being left comes up.

"Dad?"

He stubs out his cigarette and stands up. "Wherever she is, it's where she chose to be."

He walks over to the rack and takes his jacket.

"Where are you going?"

"I need a walk."

"No, Dad. I want to talk. Why are you being so dismissive?"

"Dismissive? You mean dismissive like walking away from your partner and child? That kind of dismissive?" He punches his arms into his jacket sleeves. "What do you want me to say? Your mother may now live in Spain, or Italy, or fucking Western Samoa?"

"I don't know."

He reaches past me and grabs his typed pages.

"What difference does it make, Mars? She left us."

He goes to touch my shoulder, stops himself, then leaves.

I listen to his footsteps on the stairs. Then silence. Then the slam of the shop door.

My father. Supposed grown-up.

Still hiding from questions.

After all this time.

I lock the shop and sit upstairs with a coffee.

The fridge was empty and I'm hungry. For food and answers.

The rain's started again, so, wherever Dad is, he's getting wet. Karma.

Picture him standing under a tree, staring out like a forlorn character from a Wes Anderson film, soggy pages pinned under his arm.

Is it raining in Cornwall?

Must've left my phone at home.

What updates has Cara sent?

What's she doing? Did Sean speak to Jordan?

The typewriter stares at me. I stroke the keys.

The lines that make letters. The shapes that make stories.

Could I write one?

Do I have that in me?

Everything quiet. I feel alone.

Raindrops tap-tap on the windowsill.

"Where are you, Thor Baker?"

Tap. Tap.

The two-syllable echo of Mum's name.

Tap. Tap.

Ro bin.

My head hurts.

Ro bin.

"Shut up."

Tap. Tap.

Ro bin.

I smack the table.

"Wherever you are, shut the fuck up!"

Tap. Tap. Tap.

It's not the rain. It's the door.

His wet hair is bin-bag black.

"Sorry," he says as I let him in. "No umbrella."

Same outfit as the other day. He's holding a shopping bag.

I close the door.

"Nice hair," he says, wiping water from his face. "Suits you."

My hand instinctively comes up to cover it. "Yeah, thanks."

"I was just at the supermarket, and thought I'd pop in and check, about the book? I didn't hear from you. Was that there before?"

He points at the old sofa.

"No. It's . . . we're trying something."

"I like it."

"Your book hasn't arrived yet, sorry."

"Oh, OK." He looks down at himself.

"I could check the computer," I say. "Sometimes they put an estimated date."

I walk to the till, expecting you to step out from behind the pillar and start in on him again.

You don't.

When I turn round, he has his wet jacket off. I can see a folded baguette through the opaque plastic bag.

"It's supposed to be June," he says, and it's the kind of banal line of small talk you would never give the cool older brother character.

I check the orders screen. "*Self Help*, Lorrie Moore?"

Morgan walks over. "It's not what you think. It's short stories. Amazing short stories."

"And you lost your copy?"

"You could say that. Does it give a date?"

"No. Sorry. It doesn't normally take this long. I can probably sort out a discount?"

"Don't worry about it. I'm just replacing important stuff. No rush. It'll come when it comes. Is your dad in?"

"He's gone for a walk. Clear his head."

We both look out at the heavy rain. Morgan nods. "Cleansing."

Then my stomach growls, the kind of long, embarrassing hunger growl that always seems to happen in assembly or exams or when you're stuck in an empty bookshop with your best friend's older brother.

Morgan looks down at his carrier bag, then at me.

"Hungry?"

☆

Rain pelts down.

I'm soaked through. Knock again.

"Will you open the door, please?"

Blue's shed is small enough to probably smash with one good charge. The massive Wayne-Manor-style mansion she refuses to sleep in casts a moody shadow from the top of the gravel driveway.

"Blue! Come on, let me in."

"Go away, Thor," she says from inside, and part of me wants to just pull the door off.

"I didn't know I could be called, honestly. It's the house."

"I don't care. Leave me alone."

"Blue, please. I'm soaked."

Nothing.

"Fine! Stay in your stupid little shed. You don't understand anyway."

I turn to leave. The wooden door flies open.

"Don't understand?" She's in a black vest and jeans, her hair down, brushing her shoulders. "I think I understand just fine, Thor."

"It's not what you think, Blue. Let me explain."

"There's nothing to explain. You're a puppet. Waiting to be thrown in the bin, and I'm done with picking up the pieces."

She goes to slam the door shut again, but I step forward and block it with my boot. "Wait . . ." I say.

"Move your foot, Baker, I'm not joking."

Her eyes are full of anger and we both know what she's capable of doing.

"Maybe you're right," I say, moving my foot back. "Maybe I am a puppet. But isn't that what I'm supposed to be?"

Blue shakes her head. "You're supposed to be whatever you want. Whatever makes you happy."

"And are you happy, Blue? Here? Pretending you're not a princess?"

"At least I know what I'm not. I'm nobody's lapdog, running alongside them, praying for a pat on the head. You have a life here, Thor. People who love you, and you're risking it all."

I look at my feet.

"Maybe I don't understand," she says. "I wasn't sent away, I get that, but you think what you're going through is any harder than what me or anyone else had to? You think it's easy to have the person who made you just forget you exist?"

"I never said that."

"You have a choice, Thor. Do you understand what a luxury that is?"

I look up. "And what if that choice tears me in half, Blue? What kind of luxury is that?"

Blue's eyes turn cold.

"I'd rather be torn in half than forgotten."

And she closes the door.

☆

You're fourteen.

You and Cara are getting dressed after PE.

Ten laps of the soggy school field for cross-country. Cara hung back with you: she knows you hate running. Everyone else lapped the pair of you twice.

She's telling you about her idea for her media project. It will be a YouTube channel of satirical performance art. She's excited.

She doesn't see the way you watch her towelling her hair, fastening her bra.

She tells you she will need your help to make it really good. She wants to make the first film this weekend. Will you come with her?

You zip up your skirt, your eyes on her slender feet, her perfect toes with their chipped electric-blue nail varnish.

You tell her of course you'll come with her.

You tell her you'll go wherever she wants.

☆

The remains of a shop-floor picnic.

Looks like an archaeological dig site. Bookshop Time Team.

Morgan's on the floor, scooping the last of the hummus out of its tub with the end of the baguette. I'm on the sofa, sipping my second pineapple juice. Frankfurters. Mustard. Kettle chips. Black grapes. All destroyed. He shops well.

I lean back, belly full. If he wasn't here, I'd be undoing the top button on my jeans.

"I feel like someone punched me in the stomach," I say.

Morgan smiles with a mouth full of bread. "With a baguette fist."

He empties the juice carton into his mug and I notice the bottom of a defined bicep at the edge of his black T-shirt.

"So why psychology?" he says.

I sip. "Dunno. Makes sense, I guess."

"Wow. You sound SO excited about it, Marcie."

"I am. It'll be good. Cara'll be there too."

He gives that knowing nod that says he's reading between the lines and that he understands, and it's annoying.

"Why did you choose your degree then? Why philosophy?"

Morgan considers his answer, then shrugs. "I followed a girl."

"What?"

"Yep. They told me I could study anything, that my grades were good enough. Mum wanted me to do medicine. Then I met a girl and I fell for her. I didn't really have a plan, she did, so I followed." He trails off into a thought.

I feel awkward. This is Morgan. Cara's big brother. Sitting on the shop floor, telling me he went to university to be with a girl.

"Guess I learned my lesson," he says, reaching for his jacket.

"What lesson?"

He takes out a silver tobacco tin. "Can't hitchhike someone else's life, Marcie. You get high?"

I shake my head. "Not right now."

"No, right. Sorry."

He puts the tin back in his jacket and awkwardly folds it more than he needs to.

"Medicine would've been full on," I say, helping him out.

"Yep. It would." He puts the lid back on the empty hummus tub. "It's all full on though, isn't it, doing what you're 'supposed to do'?"

He pulls his ankles in, crossing his legs, his lost expression revealing more than a second-act soliloquy.

I look out of the window. The rain is still bucketing down and it feels like we're sitting inside a bubble.

"I'm not going back," he says.

"What?"

"To uni. There's nothing for me there."

He looks at me, and I know I'm the only person he's told.

"Are you serious?"

Then Dad bursts in, out of breath.

He's soaked through, rolled-up pages sticking out of his jacket pocket.

"Quick! I need a hairdryer!"

Morgan springs to his feet. Dad looks at him, then me, then the sofa, then the picnic.

"The hairdryer, Mars, now!"

I glance at Morgan. "We don't have a hairdryer, Dad. I think you're past that point anyway."

"It's not for me, is it?" he says, reaching inside his jacket. "It's for him."

✶

It's a kitten.

Completely black. A little furry full stop, small enough to sit in his hand.

He holds it out like baby Simba. "It's a cat."

"I can see that, Dad. Whose is it?"

"It's ours. He's soaked." He looks at Morgan. "Afternoon."

Morgan almost salutes. "Afternoon, Mr Baker."

"Mars, come on! A little help!"

I stand up. "Dad, what the hell?"

"Funniest thing – actually, not funny, not funny at all – I was walking in the woods, gathering my thoughts, and this guy was just . . . well, he had this bag."

Morgan picks up our tea-towel picnic rug. "She's gorgeous," he says, walking over to Dad and taking the kitten, wrapping it up in the towel. The kitten's miaow is more like a squeak.

Morgan holds it next to his chest, gently rubbing its body. "There you go, little one. All good."

Dad looks at me. I shrug.

"So some random guy just gave you a kitten?"

Dad wipes his face. "No, I saw him drop the bag into the water by the little bridge and walk away."

"He was trying to drown it?"

"I guess so. I couldn't just . . . what could I do? Do you have any cash on you? We should buy cat food for it."

"I have some money," says Morgan, still stroking the kitten. "They need special kitten food, it's more delicate."

"OK, great. Mars, you and Dr Dolittle go and get the food. I'll take it upstairs and give it some milk." Dad holds out his hands and Morgan passes him the swaddled kitten.

"Actually, Mr Baker, milk isn't great for them when they're this small. A bowl of water is better."

"Nonsense, son. Cats love milk – everyone knows that. I'll be upstairs. Don't be long, he's hungry."

"How the hell do you know?" I say.

"Wouldn't you be, if you'd just suffered a near-death experience? Chop-chop."

And he walks to the stairs. I look at Morgan. Morgan looks at me.

"The supermarket will have what we need," he says, picking up his jacket.

This is actually happening. I pull on my hoodie and zip it up.

Alton Towers just got a new ride.

☆

I stand in the rain and stare at the house.

The front face of a place that means nothing to most people.

Just one of many.

Another number in a line of other numbers. Nothing special.

Not even real.

Not real bricks or mortar or foam insulation.

Not real carpets or wallpaper, paint or skirting boards.

Not real windows or curtains, fittings or taps.

Just background.

Just a set.

Just a puppet.

Your puppet.

Begging to be picked up.

Man, I want to fight.

I want to fight right now.

☆

I can feel its little heart beating behind the tiny grille of its ribs.

"He likes you," says Dad, twisting the corkscrew into a bottle of red wine.

I stroke a velvety ear. "Morgan said it was a girl, Dad."

"And how does he know?"

"He seemed to know quite a bit, to be fair."

"True."

"He said he'd pop in tomorrow and check on her."

"Good for him. Are you two . . . you know?"

"What? Shut up! That's Cara's big brother!"

"So? Older man, better for someone like you, more on your level."

"Just stop talking."

He pulls on the corkscrew. "He's got the look of a searcher, that one."

"A searcher? It's not *Game of Thrones*, Dad."

"You know what I mean. Somebody looking. Slightly lost."

"Know that look well, do you?"

"You'd be good for him."

"Dad, please . . ."

"Fine. There must be someone though, right?"

Cara in a quaint cottage kitchen, laughing at Sean doing his "Hotline Bling" dance as she boils water for instant noodles.

"I'm fine by myself."

"Nobody's fine by themselves, Mars. Not for long."

He pops the cork and the kitten does a terrified backflip, then tries to burrow into my stomach.

"Sorry."

He pours wine into two purple plastic tumblers and brings one over.

"About earlier," he says. And it doesn't feel right.

"It's OK, Dad." I sip from my tumbler. The wine is cold and bitter. "Forget it."

"We can talk about her if you'd like." He sits back at the table.

"Not now," I say.

We exchange nods and drink.

The kitten is now nibbling the belt loop of my jeans.

"You should name her," Dad says.

I shake my head. "I'm no good at that stuff. I should ring Coral. Have you seen my phone?"

Dad sits back down at the table and drinks. "Nope. Good riddance, I say."

"That's great, Dad. I'll try and remember your anti-phone Zen when I'm trapped under a building."

He smiles.

"What?"

"Nothing. Just a memory." He pours himself more wine. "Come on. Name her."

"I don't know, do I? You're the writer."

"Touché, my young padawan, but I named you. It is the Jedi way for you to name your own apprentice."

The kitten has now swapped my belt loop for my finger, tiny needle teeth testing my skin.

"I should go."

Dad almost chokes on his wine. "You can't go! You have to stay over. I can't watch her on my own. She's just a baby. We'll ring Coral."

Can't remember the last time I stayed over. Not since before Diane.

I look down at the kitten happily chewing my hand, pushing with its back legs for leverage.

"Calvin!" says Dad, triumphantly.

"Calvin?"

"Yeah, like it?"

"She's a girl, Dad."

"Then she shall be a girl named Calvin. That a problem for you?"

"No, but surely Hobbes makes more sense if that's where you're going. I mean, she's a cat."

Dad waves one finger as he sips. "Hobbes isn't real. Drink up."

☆

"Thor . . ."

Something tapping the bridge of my nose, sending shocks of pain across my face. "Thor Baker?"

Can't open my eyes. Ribs screaming. Hard, cold against my back. Familiar. I'm on the floor.

"Come on, son."

It's Leyland. "Open your eyes for me, Thor."

"He knew what he was doing." The scratchy tones of Burgess from my left. Stale sweat and metal.

My eyes crack open; there's wet on my chin. Blood. My skull's pulsing like an ocean-distress beacon.

"Move away," says Leyland. "Give us room."

I start to focus. Leyland's face, straining a smile. "Silly boy."

He sits me up. Ribs are cracked. Broken maybe. Paws stiff. Humming.

I cough and the hinge of my jaw creaks. My Marcie. In the real.

"Somebody better pay me, Leyland," croaks Burgess, leaning over us in his dirty apron, tree-stump cigar hanging out of his mouth.

"I said back off." Bite in Leyland's voice.

"I have money," I say, wincing as I speak, chest squeezing my lungs. "In my bag."

High warehouse ceiling. Cloudy glass panels and pigeon shit. I can hear the murmur of other voices, a handful of people. Audience.

I came for this.

"Can we get him some water or something?" Leyland says, inspecting my face. Burgess stands up straight and he's hardly any taller. Pathetic final strands of black hair clinging to his sweaty round head.

"Him? What about Roman? You know how much money this will cost me, Leyland?"

Roman? Remember running in. Demanding to fight. Burgess telling me to wait. Me shouting. Anyone. Anyone.

He was big. Much bigger. He laughed at me. His big yeti grin.

I showed him, Marcie.

He's not laughing now.

"Forget it. Can you stand?" Leyland pulls me up before I can answer. Pain skips down my back in needle high heels. Gut wrenches. Gonna puke.

Gonna puke.

Puke.

"Jesus!" Burgess hobbles backwards.

"We're leaving," says Leyland, moving me away from the splashed puddle. Burgess waves a fat finger. "Not until I get my money. Roman is my best guy, and look at him!"

There's a circle of people around the yeti, his big head propped up on a jacket. Blood. His long hairy feet limp. He'll be out for a while.

I point to my bag on the floor. Leyland hands Burgess a roll of notes from his own pocket, scoops up my bag, then throws my arm over his shoulder.

"I have money, Leyland."

"Shut up, Thor."

He's much stronger than he looks. That wiry sensei strength.

Burgess counting the notes, laughing from behind us. "Crazy shit! He could've killed you!" He almost chokes on his own cackle. "Come back soon, Baker! We can make money!"

My feet are dragging. The taste of iron. Broken and bruised. "Marcie . . ."

Leyland pulling me along. "Stop talking, Thor. Save your energy."

He lets out a little chuckle. "The carrier becomes the carried, eh?"

"Marcie . . ."

The cold air of outside splashes over me. The sun's going down.

Leyland's black Ford.

"Lean here for a second." He props me against the car and opens the door.

"I can't do it, Leyland. The house."

"OK, OK. Let's go. Mind your head."

He eases me in. Pain. Daggers in my chest.

"Marcie . . ."

"Sshhhh. What were you thinking?"

Drifting. Foggy. "It's not fair, Leyland. She needs me." Door slams.

"It's just not fair."

Then everything goes black.

☆

It isn't some massive screaming match.

No melodramatic plate-smashing, soap-opera scene like people might think.

There are few words.

You're nearly twelve, sitting on the wide foam chair of the hospital waiting room, two hours of tears drying on your cheeks.

Sean's nan, Leona, is speaking to a nurse at reception, trying to get more information.

Sean is in surgery. The burning aerosol can was lodged in his chest. Punctured his lung.

I'm sitting opposite you, the strip-lit ceiling

pressing down on us like the back of a rubbish truck.

Every time you close your eyes, you see the metal firework of it shooting from the flames straight for him. The fear in his eyes. Again and again.

Regret is crawling over my skin like bugs.

I am guilt.

I want to speak, but I know this is done.

That we're finished.

Before you look at me.

And say.

"Don't you come back."

☆

"How's your head?"

Leyland puts the tray on the floor next to the sofa. I see a glass of water, two bullet-shaped white pills and a small plate of chunky beige cookies. My head is clearing, but I can feel a regular pulse in the left side of my face. Yetis can punch.

My ribs are strapped tightly, restricting my breathing. Been a while since Leyland patched me up, but he's still got it.

He winks, takes a cookie and sits down on the chair next to his kitchen door.

"Baked them myself."

"I don't like painkillers, Leyland." I shift my body to sitting and daggers stab my spine. The other guy, Roman. Smashed him up pretty good.

For what?

Leyland bites his cookie. "Don't start that again. We've been here before, haven't we?"

"If I'm hurt, I'm hurt," I say. "The pain is mine."

"Ladies and gentlemen, your idiot king."

He wipes crumbs from his chin. "Come on then. Speak."

I ball fists and the bones in my paws creak like split floorboards. "Nothing to say."

"Allow me to grease the verbal wheels then, my young brick-brained friend. This is where you once again attempt to validate your actions by spinning some pseudo-gladiatorial romance. How, in dealing with your insurmountable frustration, somehow the only thing that makes sense is getting smashed in the face. Am I close?"

He takes another bite of cookie. I can feel the acid in my stomach.

"You don't know everything, old man."

He crosses one leg over the other like teachers do. "This is true. Everything, I do not know, but you, Thor Baker, you I know very well."

I look across at his desk. The old book-making equipment abandoned mid-job.

"I've been with her, Leyland. There. In the real."

Leyland takes a deep breath, then sings, "I've been with her, over there, her perfect lips, her Afro hair."

"Forget it." I go to stand; my skeleton shrieks; I sit back down. *Marcie.*

"Easy there, Maximus. Just a touch of banter. Forgive me. Take the pills. Eat a cookie."

I let my chin drop on to my chest. "It's too hard. I can't do it."

Leyland finishes his cookie and stands up. "A choice that is easy is no choice at all."

He walks over to his stereo and thumbs through stacked vinyl. I bite into a cookie. Soft, buttery sweetness and a hint of something else.

Low swelling strings. Dramatic but warm.

"It's the house, correct?" he says, sitting back down. "Your final test?"

"Yeah."

I take another bite.

Leyland nods. "Touché, ye gods of fate."

And suddenly I'm swallowing back the urge to cry. The pressure builds in my chest. My throat tightens. I close my eyes.

Leyland crouches in front of me and lays a hand on my knee.

"There, there, my boy. Cry if you need to. No shame in it. No shame at all."

I grit my teeth, fighting it, trying to swallow them back.

He sits down next to me on the sofa and takes out his cigarettes.

"Death, so called, is a thing which makes men weep, and yet a third of life is passed in sleep."

And I can't stop the tears.

They come flooding out with a roar.

☆

The room is leaning.

I close my eyes and try to focus on the cool air cutting in through the crack of open window.

"Call me Ishmael!" slurs Dad from the sofa, raising his tumbler like a drunken sea captain.

"That whale, Mars. That stupid fucking whale."

I stare at my empty tumbler. Feel the wine in my belly. What's Cara doing? Did Sean tell Jordan? Did Jordan make a move? Is he making a move right now?

"*Pssst.*" Dad's beckoning me over, his eyes closed. "I want to tell you something."

Standing up, I feel the weight drop into my feet.

Calvin scampers up on to the arm of the sofa, waiting for a stroke. I rub her neck and sit on the floor. "What is it?"

"Closer," says Dad, almost whispering, like he's a wizard, about to reveal a secret to his apprentice.

I kneel over him. "What?"

"You'll never do it," he says. The booze on his breath.

"I'll never do what?"

"Whatever it is that you want to do." He raises his empty glass. "Never. Gonna. Happen."

I feel my stomach twisting, wrapping itself round my spine.

"And what is it that you think I want to do, Karl?" I say, squeezing my tumbler.

Dad's eyes close.

"Dad?"

I poke his stomach and his tumbler tips over on his chest, spilling the last drops of dark wine on to his white vest.

"Dad?"

He starts to snore like a post-banquet Viking. I take the empty tumbler from his hand.

"Exactly."

Calvin walks up his body and starts sniffing the spilled wine. I pick her up and hold her in my lap.

"I'll never do it, Calvin?"

She presses her face into my fingers, demanding more strokes.

I hold her up so our noses are touching.

"It's already done."

☆

I can still feel my ribs, but there's less pain and more an awareness that they're there. I have ribs. Ribs. And I never noticed how funny that word is.

"*Riiiiiiibssss.*"

Leyland's cookies should come with a warning.

I step out of the lift. Touch my face. Really enjoying touching my face. What time is it? Feels late. I can hear my heartbeat. The *lub dub* of aortic and pulmonary valves. A-level Human Biology.

Don't know how long I cried for. Or what I said.

Have to let go. I remember Leyland saying that. Final test.

Time to move on.

He's right.

Have to let go.

Will let go.

"I will let go!"

I stick my arm out like Hamlet. "Alas, poor Thor! I knew him, Horatio."

"Shut up!" a voice shouts from inside one of the other flats.

"You shut up!"

No response.

"Yeah! Thought so! I'm Thor Baker and I'll smash your cookie! I mean face!"

I laugh and fall over.

The floor is more comfortable than I imagined. I could sleep here.

The ceiling is the same dull colour as the walls.

Somebody should paint this grey place.

Somebody should paint it every colour in the universe.

I'll do it.

When this is over, I'll buy paint and I'll throw up the whole Milky Way and make this dull place sing.

I'm fine. Time to move on.

"Time to move on, Marcie!" I bang the wall. "Everyone! It's time to move on!"

"Shut up!" calls the voice again.

"Who said that? Come out here and say it!"

I sit up and the corridor spins.

"I'll smash everything! You hear me? It's what I do!"

It's what I do.

In fact, it's what I'm going to do. Right now.

I push myself up using the wall.

And smack the button for the lift.

☆

"Mars?"

"Yeah, it's me."

"What's this number?"

"The shop. I'm in the shop. Shoppy, shop shop."

"It's nearly one o'clock, Mars."

"Is it? When did that happen?"

"Are you sleeping there? Where's your phone?"

"Can't find it. How's it going?"

"So you didn't get my texts? My message?"

"No. What did they say?"

"They said it's all gone weird. Sean's being well funny with me."

"Funny how?"

"I dunno, just funny."

"Funny like a clown? Like I'm here to amuse you?"

"Are you OK?"

"We got a cat. Where are you now?"

"Are you drunk?"

"No. Yes. So? Are you on the beach?"

"Haha! You're drunk!"

"No I'm not. I'm good. I'm great. I'm gravy. Where's Sean?"

"I don't know. I'm in bed."

"With Jordan?"

"What? Shut up! Why would you even say that?"

"I dunno. Holidays. Stuff happens. We called her Calvin, the cat. Oh no."

"What? Are you OK? Mars?"

"I threw up a little bit in my mouth."

"Who are you with? Are you on your own? Marcie?"

"I want to tell you something."

"Tell me what?"

"I'm sorry, Car."

"What for?"

"I'm really sorry."

"Marcie, who's there with you?"

"I miss you."

"I miss you too. Marcie? Are you still there?"

"Yeah."

"I dunno. Maybe I'm completely misreading him. I can't gauge it. I wish you were here to tell me."

"I need to tell you."

"Tell me what?"

"Hi."

"*Hi.*"

"High? Are you stoned? Did you smoke with your dad?"

"You took your time."

"*Sorry.*"

"I almost told her."

"*Not yet.*"

"Marcie, who are you talking to? Is your dad there?"

"He's sleeping."

"So you're on your own? Marcie?"

"No. I'm not on my own."

"What? Who's there? Mars?"

"I have to go, Car."

"Are you OK?"

"I'm fine. I'm with the cat. I need to drink some water."

"Good idea. And eat some toast."

"Yeah. Night night."

"OK. Drink lots. Call me tomorrow. And find your phone!"

You take up most of the doorway.

Light from the stairs sends your shadow across the shop floor towards me.

The boy with bear arms.

I hang up.

I can't see your face but I feel your stare. My head is swimming.

Your broad shoulders rise and fall.

"I couldn't do it, Marcie."

Neither of us moves.

"Couldn't do what?"

"What I'm supposed to."

I step from behind the counter. I can feel my heartbeat.

"Maybe you don't have to."

☆

We sit in the back room.

You on the bed, me in the desk chair facing you.

The glass flower lamp is our little campfire.

The cookies are wearing off and my ribs feel a lot less funny now.

I meant to smash. I did. I was going to knock the whole front of the house clean off. I was.

But I couldn't.

"Am I allowed to know what happened to your face?" you say.

And I shouldn't. But I don't care.

"*I was in a fight.*"

"With who?"

I have to smile. "*A yeti.*"

You don't laugh, sitting forward, taking in my bruise.

"You fight a lot, don't you?"

"*Sometimes. Used to a lot more.*"

"Angry."

"*Yeah.*"

"I think you took my temper with you, when you left."

"*I didn't leave.*"

I can feel my bones now. Raw and aching.

"There's so much you don't know, Marcie. So much you can't."

My skull feels like it might split in two at any second. I press my face into my paws in case it does.

"You're hurt bad," you say, standing up. I watch you wobble slightly.

"And you're drunk."

"Three glasses of wine. Not exactly Lindsay Lohan, am I?"

You smile, and everything that matters is right in front of me.

That's the truth.

"Come here," you say.

I stand up, gritting my teeth from the pain.

"Where does it hurt?"

"My ribs, mostly."

You step forward and put your hand on my chest. "Here?"

I nod.

You take my paws in your hands and shake your head.

"It doesn't hurt any more."

"*What?*"

"It doesn't hurt any more."

"*Marcie, I . . .*"

Then I feel a heat. You close your eyes and squeeze my paws and something is spreading through them, up along my arms. Something golden.

"*What are you doing?*" I say. But it feels amazing. Like the inside of my arms are filling up with thick, warm honey, smothering the pain.

It reaches my elbows. My shoulders. I'm watching your face. Your tongue is sticking out like a little pink flag, the way it used to when you'd draw. The warmth reaches my chest. The pain. Fading. You're healing me, from the inside. My ribs. My neck.

I am floating with my feet on the floor. Close my eyes. Breathe in. Breathe out. And open.

You're looking up at me, your hands still gripping my paws.

"I missed you, Thor Baker."

You smile again, and every single cell in my body smiles back.

Then you stumble forward

and I catch you.

All your weight in my arms.

"I missed you too, my Marcie. So much."

I can hear you breathing.

You are fast asleep.

SATURDAY

(4 DAYS LEFT)

Somebody scraped my stomach out with a dinner fork.

The same person pushed barbed wire into the marrow of all of my bones and shrank my skull to suffocate my brain.

Sandpaper scratches my chin. A low purring.

I open my eyes to Calvin, sitting on my chest, licking my face like I taste nice.

I'm in the back room. It's too bright.

My jeans, socks and shoes are folded neatly on the floor. I lift Calvin and check under the blanket. I'm in my knickers and T-shirt, bra still on, cutting into my ribs. Flash of your face. Close. Blurry. Cara?

I swallow, and my mouth tastes like athlete's foot. I need Nurofen.

Calvin tumbles into my lap as I sit up. The desk chair

is turned to face me. Empty. The picture you drew of Coral's house still looks like a robot.

Calvin starts pawing at my thighs through the blanket like she's kneading pizza dough. I stroke between her shoulder blades and she rolls over.

"What happened, Calvin?"

She nuzzles her face on my fingers, her body vibrating with each purr.

Then something stirs in my stomach and I'm up, running to the bathroom, covering my mouth.

TWO LITRES OF WATER, 400MG OF NUROFEN, TWO TEETH-BRUSHINGS AND ONE TWENTY-FIVE-MINUTE SHOWER LATER . . .

"Feeling delicate?" says Dad, stretched out on the sofa, cigarette in hand, still in his clothes from yesterday. Calvin is sleeping at his bare feet, something violiny playing quietly through the shelf speakers.

"Yeah. You?"

"I'm OK," he says. "Good to kill a few brain cells once in a while. Dead wood."

"Well, I'm dead wood all over."

I pull up the collar on his dark dressing gown. "She seems peaceful."

Dad smiles at Calvin. "She peed in my shoes." The dark wine stain on his chest looks like he was shot with an arrow.

"There's coffee in the pot," he says, holding up his mug, and waking up in the same place as him feels strange. It hasn't happened for so long. I like it.

The pills are working, but it still feels like my stomach has turned itself inside out. I'm never drinking again.

Then the phone rings downstairs.

Dad looks at me and shrugs. "Nobody I know has the number."

The shrill ring bounces round the empty shop.

Cara's number is written in Sharpie on the top Post-it note next to the till. It's the only number I know off by heart. That's how I phoned her. What did I say?

I stare at the phone until it stops.

I look at the shelves. Books stare back at me like a judgemental amphitheatre audience. Whatever I did, they saw it all.

I turn to go back upstairs, and the phone starts again. Cara doesn't accept defeat easily.

"Car?" My throat is sore from throwing up.

"Marcie?"

It's Coral.

"Yeah?"

"I need you to come home."

"What's wrong? Are you OK?"

"Just come home, now."

"I'm not feeling very well, Coral."

"Don't give me that. Get your dad to drive you." She calls out to someone. "Yes, I'm coming!"

"Coral?"

"Do you hear me, Mars?"

"What's going on? Who are you speaking to?"

"Home, young lady. Now!"

☆

Sitting on the landing. Staring at your door.

I can still feel your hands on my paws.

That sounds like a song.

I wish I could sing.

*

Should be with Alan now.

Picture him staring across his desk at the empty chair.

I remember something Leyland said to me near the end of my first week. It was the first time he'd taken me out on to the roof. The pink and purple stripes of a Fridge City sunset. Cradling the mug of hot chocolate he'd made me.

"Rules have reason, Thor," he said in his grandmaster voice, tapping out a cigarette, "but all reason begs argument."

I remember trying to pull a serious expression, pretending to understand. Leyland could clearly sense my confusion.

"Just because something was there before us," he added, smiling, "doesn't mean it can't be wrong."

I think that's what he said. Long time ago now.

Last night happened. The way you looked at me.

Before you passed out. Before I put you into bed.

Whatever that was, it felt good, didn't it, Marcie?

Good enough not to give up.

No matter what the rules say.

☆

There's a white van outside the house, and the front door is open.

Dad leaves the engine running. I still feel rough.

"Say hi from me," he says.

"You're not coming in?"

"I don't think so, Mars. Can't face big sister with this headache."

Then Nick Fury comes out, pulling a suitcase.

I get out.

"Dom? What's going on?"

"Who's that?" says Dad.

Dom does a double take when he sees my hair.

"You better speak to your aunt."

The bath is in the kitchen.

Everything is soaked with water, the table is completely

smashed, there's plaster and rotten wood everywhere and, through the dripping hole where the ceiling used to be, you can see up into the bathroom. It looks like a tidal wave hit the house.

A chunky, sunburnt man with a shaved head and an Aston Villa shirt is shovelling soggy debris into a metal wheelbarrow. Past him, through the open patio doors, Coral is sitting outside, smoking a cigarette.

"Holy shit!" says Dad. "What happened?"

The chunky guy stops shovelling. "Flooded," he says, pointing up at the hole.

"Somebody left the sink tap running with the plug in, and the toilet was blocked. Must've been going all yesterday and last night, old floorboards couldn't take it. Lucky no one was in. I'm Pat."

He holds out his hand. Dad shakes it, staring up through the hole.

"Someone left a tap running?" I say.

Pat points out at Coral. "Better speak to her."

Dom comes back down the hall. "Did you call the skip?" he says to Pat.

Pat nods. "'Bout an hour."

Dom looks at Dad. "You must be Karl. I'm Dom."

Dad looks at me as he shakes Dom's hand.

"I'm gonna need some room here," says Pat, trying to reverse the full wheelbarrow.

Dom and Dad back up down the hall. I squeeze past Pat and step over the wet rubble to the patio doors.

Coral smokes like a movie star.

Taking long drags, she stares down the garden. I haven't seen her with a cigarette in years.

"Are you OK?" I say, not sitting down.

Coral doesn't answer.

"Coral?"

She nods to herself. "I was going to do sea bass."

"Pardon?"

"For dinner. I watched that Rick Stein guy – he did this sea bass, simple really, olive oil, lemon, bit of parsley." She takes a drag. "Little rocket salad."

"Coral . . ."

"Ten thousand, he thinks." Her lips shake as she exhales.

"What, pounds?"

She looks at me. "Yes, Marcie. Pounds."

"Man . . ."

"I only popped back for my glasses this morning, on my way to the market. I forgot them yesterday."

I sit down. "Good that you were at Dom's, right?"

"Where's your phone?" she says.

"No idea. Somewhere upstairs probably, forgot it yesterday. What's that?"

She's holding up a plastic sandwich bag, cloudy with condensation.

Inside, lifeless, is my phone.

"He said it must've flipped on its side and blocked the U-bend."

"But he said it was the sink."

"It was the sink. But he found that too."

"I don't understand. How did it . . .?"

She stares at me. Are you watching this? Can you see?

"It's going to take a couple of weeks, he says. The whole floor needs replacing before he can fit a new suite."

"Coral, I don't remember leaving the tap on, and I only realised I couldn't find my phone in the afternoon. I didn't know it had happened. Honestly."

Your face. That smile.

"Dom's offered to let us stay with him," Coral says,

stubbing out her cigarette. “While it’s being done, seeing as how we’ll have no access to the kitchen, or a bathroom.”

My phone, in the bag, like a dead fairground fish.

You did this.

“Coral . . .”

“Just tell me, Marcie. Tell me it was an accident.”

“Coral, I swear. I didn’t know. I’m so sorry.”

The doubt in her eyes.

That hollow, broken feeling.

How long has it been?

Years.

And yet it still feels exactly the same.

☆

I feel the call.

The buzz in the pit of my stomach. The crackle up my spine.

Staring at your bedroom door, I smile and let the light fill me up.

What will you say, about last night? What did that feeling mean?

Something good.

I know you felt it.

Close my eyes. Feel myself crossing.

I'm so excited, Marcie.

Me and you.

☆

A pigeon flutters above us in the bandstand rafters. I don't speak.

Down the slope, near the playground, a little girl in a white dress is chasing a red ball across the grass while her mother lays out a picnic blanket next to their buggy.

The girl trips and falls on to the ball, trapping it under her.

Her mother calls out, worried.

The girl pushes herself back up like a tiny weightlifter, holding the ball above her head, smiling proudly. Her mother applauds as the little girl runs back to the blanket.

Will either of them remember this moment?

Will either one of their brains, capable of storing everything that ever happened, choose to put this perfect short film on one of the shelves they regularly browse?

What will they remember? A colour? A facial expression? A feeling?

I have a shelf in my mind for my mother, and most of it is empty space.

"Marcie, please . . ."

"What if Coral had been home, Thor? What if she'd been in the kitchen?"

You can't look at me.

"I don't know."

"What don't you know? That she would've been squashed? My only aunt, flattened? Look at me!"

The guilt on your face.

"Why did you do it?"

Acid bubbling in my stomach.

"I never meant to hurt anyone, Marcie. I swear! It was just . . . there. I can't explain. I didn't plan it. It just happened."

I sip from my water bottle and stare at you, guilt and anger mixing with the bile.

"Nobody else is getting hurt. You understand me?"

"Marcie . . ."

"Don't speak. Don't you say another thing."

You look down, dejected, paws in your lap.

"It's not fair, Thor. You understand that, don't you? Thor!"

Then you growl. A low rumble, and I watch your paws ball into fists.

"Fair? What do you know about fair, Marcie Baker?"

"What?"

"You don't know anything at all."

And you're gone.

I stare at the silent space where you were, somehow louder than a scream.

☆

Feels like someone has their hands around my throat.

The dark hall. Your bedroom door.

Fair?

My head is spinning.

Stumble towards Coral's room. I see spots, like fireflies, hovering.

Not fair?

I push against the wall either side of her door to steady myself. Force my breath out. Press my feet into the floor.

Close my eyes.

Fair?

Push my full weight against the wall.

Not fucking fair?

Nobody's getting hurt?

Push.

What about last night? Push.

I know you felt it.

Fire fills my arms. Lava in my legs.

Nobody else is getting hurt?

What about Thor Baker, Marcie?

Burning.

Push.

Fire.

What about me?

Open my eyes.

And smash.

☆

Dad and Morgan are deep in discussion at the till, looking like some crappy eighties cop duo. Morgan's distressed T-shirt for the day is dirty white; Dad's vest/open-shirt combo is set in stone. The old man who's in love with Diane is sitting on the sofa, reading a thick hardback.

"Here she is!" says Dad. "The demolisher of houses!"

The old guy looks up from his book. His mouth falls open when he sees my hair.

Morgan laughs along with Dad. My stomach is still churning.

"That's not funny," I say, and they both stop. "Where's my stuff?"

"In the back room," says Dad, like a little kid who's just been told off. "Calvin's guarding it. New phone?" He points at my Carphone Warehouse bag.

"Yep. Coral's orders."

"She'll cool down, Mars. Give her a day or two."

I feel like I'm going to puke.

Morgan holds up a pale book with a picture of medicine cabinet shelves on the front.

"It came," he says, like I've been holding my breath for it to arrive.

"Brilliant," I say, and walk through to the back.

Calvin is trying to destroy what looks like the brown skeleton of a small Christmas tree. She's got it pinned on its side, front paws holding it while her back paws pummel it like a little UFC fighter. I push the chunky suitcase against the wall, plug my new phone in to charge and lie down.

Close my eyes.

Your face. Hurt and angry.

Coral's face. Hurt and angry.

Dad and Dom sitting on the sofa, both trying to hold the strongest posture. Dom saying he has room for me and Coral. Dad shaking his head, saying I can stay with him. Coral unsure. Dad puffing his chest.

Breathe.

It's been a while since I felt like the eye of the storm.

"It's a scratching post." Morgan's voice makes me jump.

"Sorry, didn't mean to scare you. I found it in the shed at home."

"You didn't scare me." I sit up. We both watch Calvin.

"Why's she trying to kill it?"

Morgan smiles, leaning on the door frame, book in his hand, a little too familiar.

"It's full of catnip."

"What?"

"Crack for cats."

Calvin stops for a second and looks at us, like she knows we're talking about her, then flicks back into attack mode.

"So who are you then?" I say. "The cat crack dealer? Turning innocent kittens into fiends?"

Morgan rubs his hands together. "Oh yeah, Big Daddy Morgan got the juice. Gotta get my tricks high, before I put 'em out on the streets!"

I shake my head.

"Too much?" he says.

"Yeah."

"Sorry."

My new phone pings. Then again. And again.

Unreceived messages transferring from the Cloud.

"Somebody likes you," says Morgan, like he's auditioning for the role of cheesy, middle-aged uncle.

"You and Dad getting along then?" I say, tipping the suitcase on to its side at my feet and unzipping it.

"He's a genius," says Morgan, without even a slither of sarcasm, and I kind of wish you were here, just to shoot him down.

"So they say." I take my laptop out and put it on the bed.

Morgan steps into the room. "Do you write too?"

"No."

"You used to draw though, right? I remember that."

He looks at your robot face house on the wall. "Still decent with the pen."

Embarrassment rising. "I didn't draw that."

My folded clothes stacked like lasagne, white bra poking out. I hurriedly tuck it back in and close the suitcase as Morgan walks to the desk. My headache's coming back with a vengeance.

"You didn't fancy the seaside then?" he says, looking at Diane's books.

Why's he here? What does he want?

"Dad needs me to help with the shop," I say.

"Course. And you've got your demolition work too, right?"

He grins, and it's like a glimpse into the annoying side of having an older brother. Walking into your space uninvited, commenting on your life.

I hear your voice.

"What do you want, Morgan?"

He looks at me, shocked. "Sorry. I didn't mean to just barge in. I'll go."

He stops when he reaches the door. "Is he working on something new, your dad?"

"Apparently. Why don't you ask him?"

Morgan gives the door frame a pathetic tap.

"I guess when you're trying to follow up something perfect, you can't rush, right?"

"Guess not."

Calvin is running out of steam, throwing laboured punches at her post.

"It is perfect, isn't it?" Morgan says. "*Dark Corners . . .*"

I look at him. "Super-cool" big brother Morgan. Philosophy brainbox. Blatant fanboy.

"I wouldn't know," I say. "I haven't read it."

☆

Wipe my mouth and look down.

The upstairs wall is now a pile of rubble in the front yard below me. I'm sitting on the edge of the floor where the wall between Coral's room and the spare room used to be. The entire upper-front quarter of the house is now gone. I smile proudly and look both ways along the quiet early evening

street. There's nobody around, except the little black cat who didn't want to be stroked, sitting on the metal bin outside next door.

"Look what I did," I say, smiling down at it.

The cat stares back up, unimpressed.

I swig the last of my milk from the bottle and hold it out in front of me like a crane.

"Geronimo!"

The glass shatters on the pile of bricks, sending a fountain of shards sprinkling out and the cat running under next-door's hedge.

You can't beat a good smash.

I lean back for my bag and the floorboards creak underneath me. Only the central walls are load-bearing, so, if I work on the downstairs front tomorrow, the back half should stay secure enough to do the back roof next. Whole thing shouldn't take more than a couple of days. I'll have time to spare.

Who's in charge now, Marcie?

The floor underneath me creaks again and my eyes go blurry.

Shake my head. Feel myself leaning, chest tightening.

There's a loud crack, then the shattering of glass as the front downstairs window caves in. The floor groans.

The fireflies are back. Spots of light in the haze.

I try to swat them away and fall forward, off the edge of the house.

As it collapses beneath me.

☆

Went in sea! Freezing! X

Creepy cafe. Old English women looking at us like aliens. Well UKIP. What even is a scone? X

Sean being funny with me maybe x can't tell

Sean def funny. Avoiding talking to me. Can you speak? X

8 Missed Calls.

Where are you Mars? X

Yo. You sure bout Cara and J? Sean

You have two new messages. First message received yesterday at thirteen nineteen:

"It's gone weird, Mars. I'm getting mixed signals, like stupidly mixed. God. I know your phone's probably under your bed or in the washing machine or something, but, when you find it, call me, OK?"

Second message received today at eight twenty-four:

"It's me. Morning. Hope you're not feeling too rough? What were you drinking? Hope you've found your phone; if you're listening to this, you must have. Unless you're not Marcie and you're some weirdo phone thief who gets off on listening to other people's messages, in which case I hope your dick drops off and you lose your memory. Sorry, Mars. Just in case. Woke up feeling different. Think I might be misreading things with Sean. Think it's fine. Wish you were here to tell me. Call me when you can. Miss you."

Can't face calling her. Don't know what I'd say. Tell her the truth?

Truth hurts.

So does my head.

"Quite a day, eh?"

Dad's holding two mugs.

I shake my head. "Not up to coffee, Dad."

"It's not coffee."

He hands me a mug and sits down at the desk. "Did you text Coral?"

"Yeah."

"She'll be fine. It'll give her a chance to road-test whatshisname."

"Dom. He seems nice."

"He'll need to be more than nice to tick my sister's boxes."

I take a deep breath of the hot chocolate and I'm seven. Sitting in my bedroom in the old house, before Coral's, sipping from one of the big mugs as he tells me that mum's gone on "a trip".

"Eighteen soon, Mars," he says. "Can you believe it?"

I run my finger round the foamy edge of my mug. "Kind of have to, don't I?"

"You'll be fine."

"Yeah? What makes you so sure?"

He stares into his chocolate. "Because you're strong enough to do what you want."

Younger Dad, sitting on my bedroom floor, all weak smiles and no answers.

"Doesn't suit you," I say.

"What doesn't?"

"Fatherly wisdom."

I watch his eyes glaze over, like somebody took out his batteries. Then he smiles.

"You're right. Who am I kidding?"

"Not me."

We sit and sip quietly by lamplight.

"You want to know what she wrote, in the letter?"

"Mars . . . I—" He shakes his head. He still can't handle it.

I lean back against the wall. Dad looks down. "I'm sorry," he says.

His face is all apology, like he's been saving them up, waiting for the right moment.

"I remember fighting," I say. "Hearing you fight. Stuff smashing."

Dad sits back. "Yeah. She liked to throw stuff. Used to make her so angry."

"What did?"

"Me. I wasn't what she wanted."

He finishes his chocolate and wipes the foam from his lips.

"People do what they want, Mars, or they don't. Nobody knows what'll make them happy. Not until they find it."

He smiles and stands up and, even though part of me wants more, it feels like the end of the scene.

"She seems peaceful," he says, pointing at Calvin fast asleep at the end of the bed.

"She's knackered," I say. "And high. Morgan made sure of that."

"He seems like a good guy. How old is he?"

"Twenty, I think. Why?"

"No reason."

"I'm not interested in Morgan, Dad."

"I know you're not." He points at my black ink line on the wall. "You going to finish that?"

I sip the last of my chocolate. "Dunno. Maybe."

"Ideas come when they're ready. Not before," he says.

I wipe the ring of chocolate from inside my mug and lick my finger.

"He's a big fan of yours, you know, Morgan?"

Dad shakes his head,. "He clearly doesn't have a clue what he is, that one. Warm boy though, good with people."

"Yeah? Why don't you give him a job then?" I say smiling.

Dad taps his empty mug on the door frame.

"I did. He starts Monday."

☆

Step out of the lift.

The cast on my left arm looks like the end of a giant cotton bud. My back is killing me, and my forehead still stings.

It was already dark when I came to, spreadeagled on a mound of broken bricks, and, by the time I got myself to the hospital, the waiting room was full of drunken Saturday night casualties.

Nobody else is getting hurt.

It's the fade, I know that. Seeing spots. The weakness.

The house has no front now. An open 3D cross-section model of the place you grew up in. I'm the best at my job even by accident.

I just want bed.

The bin bag is still outside next door. Black and slumped.

"Why the hell are you still here?" Their door is closed.

"This isn't a rubbish dump, you know. You hear me?" I step towards it. "You stupid sack of useless rubbish."

My body aches.

"What did you say?"

The bag sits lifeless.

"Yeah. Thought so. Stay quiet. We're nothing alike."

Kick my door open. And shuffle inside.

SUNDAY

(3 DAYS LEFT)

Sundays slow the world down.

Everything takes longer. Breathing. The kettle boiling. Lights blinking on.

It's like, for the rest of the week, the record spins at forty-five rpm, but on Sunday somebody switches the turntable to thirty-three.

I pull the sheet up over my shoulders. Everything is asleep.

It's the prologue to the day.

This is the hour when you can hear the invisible veins of a house, the pipes that bring the heat and the water. It's the hour when people who are awake sit, with hot drinks, staring out of windows, thinking about important things.

About leaving.

*

She'll be awake.

She'll be sitting at a thick wooden table, in some long, Spanish barn-conversion kitchen, dropping blueberries into a bowl of bright white yoghurt. Pushing her hair behind her ear and reaching for the jar of locally sourced honey.

There'll be a dog. Near her bare feet. One of those big horsey dogs that lollops around on chunky paws. The kind of dog more likely to lick a burglar's hand than raise the alarm.

And music. Low and warm. Something that feels obvious. Nina Simone or Ella Fitzgerald, but to her it will have special meaning. Like she couldn't get to sleep as a baby without being sung "Miss Otis Regrets".

She'll sip her coffee, from one of those chic, retro glass mugs, and stare out through the open back door.

And there'll be a thought.

Half a thought.

A picture.

A face.

A girl.

A daughter.

☆

Stare at the phone.

Shiny black plastic. Circular dial.

Blue could fix me.

Easy as breathing, she could make the pain in my body go away.

So why don't I call her?

The phone stares back at me. Still in my clothes from yesterday. On top of my duvet. Nearly midday.

"Shut up."

I roll over and something digs into my thigh. Straining to lift my body, I pull out a chunk of brick. A cube of chipped maroon with a limpet of pale mortar stuck to the corner. Stare at it. Broken and rubbish.

Made for a purpose.

Then thrown on the pile.

☆

Four rings is the usual cut-off.

The point when I get myself ready to leave an answerphone message rather than speak to the actual person. What message do I leave? How do I sum this up in a concise and clear way before the beep? Why didn't I plan my speech before I called?

"Mars?" She's outside. The air swirling around the receiver.

"Yeah."

"What? Can you? Me? Been?"

"Car?"

"Reception. Crap. We're. These cliffs!"

"Cool,"

"What?"

"I said cool. Listen, Car—"

"So cool, Mars! Like. Postcard. Something. Tried. Phone? You doing?"

"Yeah. I wanted to speak to you. I've got something to say."

"Mars? I. Anything. Vodafone. Shit."

"Car? Cara?"

"Night. Sean. Sofa. Weird."

"Cara?"

"Mars?"

Gone.

*

They can clone a sheep. And put nano-cameras in paint.

But take a mobile phone to where the land meets the sea and you're screwed.

Grab laptop from desk.

Through to empty shop. Mini jack lead. iTunes. Empty-house playlist.

Tune Yard's "Bird-Brains". Volume up. All the way up.

Play.

Loud, warped, reversed strings pour out like rainbow-coloured lava.

Thick, plucked guitar.

Merrill Garbus's voice.

"I'll never leave you alone

Breaking is part of the bone."

☆

`Nine hundred and sixty-two pages.`

`Six years of on-and-off watching.`

`Six years of slow-motion claw typing.`

`Pointless now.`

`Three more days and this will just be a typewriter.`

My window to you will close. The house will be gone.

And all I'll have is this stupid pile of pages.

A pelican as big as an elephant lands on top of the office block across the street. Its huge feathers are a royal blue with black tips. Golden-yellow beak. Its webbed feet curl over the edge of the roof as it scours the street below. Maybe I could move. Find somewhere else. Maybe I could hitch a ride in its mouth when it takes off.

Take off.

Leave all of this behind.

Three. Two. One.

☆

"What?"

Calvin is sitting in the middle of the floor, head tilted, staring at me.

"You got something to say?"

She yawns and falls over.

I nod. "Yeah, and stay down."

The black line I drew on the wall is a single strand of

a giant's hair. A giant Cara. Jet-black bob, bending down like the BFG to look into the window of Coral's house.

I go to the filing cabinet and open the top drawer. A few office-looking papers and a pen. I take out the pen and open the second drawer. More papers, a packet of black plastic spines and two more pens. I take out the pens and spines and pull at the bottom drawer. It doesn't budge.

I pull harder. Nothing.

I take one of the spines from the packet and try to wedge it in the gap between the top of the drawer and the frame. Calvin sits up and watches me like I'm a YouTube clip.

'Girl vs Drawer.'

I manage to force the narrow end of the spine into the gap, then try to lever the drawer open, jiggling it a little further in. It won't move and now the spine is bending.

"Why lock a drawer, Calvin? Eh?"

I lean on the spine and it snaps, a small piece of black plastic stuck in the gap.

"Shit!"

I smack the drawer with the bottom of my fist and the bang makes Calvin dart out of the room.

"Easy!" says Dad's voice from the stairs and I hear him stumble down the last few, trying not to step on her as she scampers past him.

"You scared her."

I drop the broken spine. "Yeah. Sorry."

"What you doing?"

"This dumb drawer won't open."

"What's in it?"

"How should I know, Dad? It's your flipping cabinet. Why did you lock it? Top-secret documents?"

Dad stares at the filing cabinet like he's trying to read a road sign from 150 metres.

"Who knows? Diamonds? Human hand?"

"Forget it." I sit back on the bed. "How's it going then?"

Dad sighs. "Don't become a writer, Mars."

"I hadn't planned to."

"Neither did I. Budge up."

He sits down next to me, our backs against the wall. "Maybe there's enough books," he says.

If it was anyone else, it'd feel like they were fishing for compliments, but it's Dad, so it sounds more like a heavily considered argument.

I nod slowly. "Maybe. But what else can you do?"

"That, my cocktail-haired princess, is the question." He lifts his bare feet and wiggles his toes.

"What's on your mind, Mars?"

Cara. Mum. That last exam. The future. You.

"Nothing."

Then he punches my thigh. Like a proper punch, and the muscle goes numb.

"Ow! Why'd you do that?"

"Now you've got something to think about," he says.

I rub my thigh. And laugh.

He laughs too.

Both of us watching the empty chair.

MONDAY

(2 DAYS LEFT)

THOR BAKER:
FADE COUNSELLING SESSION 6
8AM

I wasn't sure you'd come.

Me either.

But you did.

Yeah.

Can I ask about the arm?

Accident, at work.

I see. And how's it going, work?

It's going.

And you?

I'm going too.

Thor . . .

I get it, Alan. It's OK. No more resisting. I'll do what you want.

This isn't about me, Thor. What do you want?

Does it matter?

Did something happen?

Nothing new.

Are you OK?

I don't know.

Do you feel it coming?

All the time.

And does it make sense to you now?

It always made sense, Alan. Just not a sense I was happy with.

I know what you mean. I'm glad you came.

Can I have some of that water?

Of course. Let me pour.

It's fizzy.

You don't like fizzy?

Tastes like farts.

Sorry. I'll get some still for next time.

We have one more session after this?

That's what the schedule says, yes.

How long did it take you, Alan? To get over it?

I'm not sure any of us ever gets "over it". I think it's more about acceptance, and then getting on with the rest of your life.

Getting on?

Yes.

Like a train.

In a manner of speaking. A train to your future.

One-way ticket.

Yep.

Last stop Death.

I wasn't going that way with it.

Imagine if they knew, Alan? Imagine if they knew about all this? All of us? You ever think that?

I've thought about it, yes. Not sure what it would change though.

Maybe it wouldn't feel so unfair.

We live for them, Thor. It's how it's always been.

I know. Doesn't make it feel any less like a defeat though, does it?

Is that what you feel, Thor? Like you're losing?

I kinda feel like I already lost.

☆

There's space on the low non-fiction shelves to stack the books from the display.

I push the empty table next to the sofa and rearrange the other three so that each one has two different categories on it. Getting rid of the symmetry seems to wake the shop up.

By the time Morgan knocks on the door at nine forty-five, the shop is fully stamped with my touch.

"It looks great!" he says, taking off his jacket. Distressed T-shirt colour for the day: marl grey.

"What do you want me to do?"

I boot up the till. "I think Dad probably wants to give the orders."

"He said that you were in charge. Told me to do whatever you said."

I look at the back door. Johnny Cash grins my way.

"Course he did. OK, have you ever worked in a bookshop before?"

"No."

"Right. But you've worked in a shop before?"

"No."

"Pub? Bar?"

He shakes his head.

"Cafe?"

"No."

"OK, so where have you worked?"

I sip the last of my cold coffee.

"Nowhere," he says with a sheepish shrug. "Never had a job."

"Ever?"

"Nope."

"Not even a summer one?"

"Pathetic, right?"

"No. Yeah. A little bit."

"Sorry."

"No need to be sorry. Your degree must be pretty full on."

"Twelve hours a week."

"That's it? Are you kidding?"

He nods sarcastically. "It was pretty tough."

"Was? So you're seriously not going back?"

"Nope."

I give him the suspicious detective glare. He just shrugs. "I'm not joking, Marcie."

"Man. What did your parents say?"

"They don't know."

"Cara?"

He shakes his head.

I knew it. This is nuts.

Picture Cara's face, twisted in confusion. Morgan's academic career was always carved in stone.

"So what? You figured you'd just work in a bookshop?"

"Would that be so bad?"

He's testing me. It's annoying.

"Whatever. It's your life." I try to bite my tongue, but I can't stop the question popping out. "Why though?"

"Lots of reasons."

"But you only had a year left."

"Yeah. Another whole year of my life that I wasn't up for wasting. I just knew I had to leave. I know that probably doesn't make any sense to someone about to set off on their own version, but . . . what's wrong?" he says, staring at me like my face is revealing something without me knowing.

"Nothing's wrong. And nobody knows?"

"Just the admin secretary and you. And Nayimah."

"Who's Nayimah?"

"One of the other reasons."

"Man. Great name."

His whole body slumps. "Yeah."

I grab my mug.

"This is too much information in one go. I need another coffee. You want a coffee?"

"Yes, please. Are you OK, Marcie?"

"I'm fine."

"Sorry to throw my shit on you. I'll shut up."

"Morgan, I'm fine. Milk?"

"No thanks, one sugar though. Is your dad upstairs? Shall I go up?"

"Nope. You've got your first shop test."

I point at the shelf of records. "Choose the music."

Morgan looks at the turntable. "All vinyl?"

"Yep," I say, stepping out of the way.

He runs his finger along the edge of the albums, then looks at me. "Sweet."

I shake my head.

"Not if you pick the wrong one. We open up in five."

☆

Stare at my punchbag.

The desire to hit it with everything I've got vs the knowledge of how much it will hurt if I do.

I give my cast a tap and a depth charge of pain ignites in my bone.

This is it. Waiting.

Wednesday will come. I'll feel something. Something weird.

Something I've never felt before. Then it'll be over.

I remember them speaking to us that first week. Temporary, they said. Made to fill a gap. Bridge a trauma. Don't expect too much, they said. A set period of time. Short-lived, and then done.

Temporary.

Like anyone's not?

Who isn't temporary? Who's permanent?

We all just brushed it off. Yeah, yeah, temporary. Whatever.

Man, the end looks different when you're close to it.

Typewriter smiles.

No. Not today. Not any more.

Stop it.

There's no point. Not for me.

`No.`

`So what?`

`It's not about me any more.`

`It's about her, isn't it?`

`Isn't it?`

☆

Fuzzy, plucked guitar, ghostly strings and scratches.

Portishead's "Mysterons". The sounds transport me back. I'm standing up in a cot, my face pressed between the bars, watching Mum and Dad read on their bed.

Morgan smiles. "So, do I pass?"

I hand him his mug and sit down behind the till.

"Decent."

He nods back like a little kid. "Thanks. Whose records are these, by the way?"

"My parents' mostly. Some of the newer ones are Diane's."

"Diane?"

"She used to work here."

"Right. So you grew up listening to this stuff?"

"Yep."

"That explains a lot."

"Like what?"

"I dunno. You always seemed . . . older."

He leans on the counter. "So I'm off to a good start?"

I point at the door. "Not if the sign says 'closed'."

I show him the till. The card machine. Stock search. He nods along, attentive and excited. And it's cool. Nice even. I feel busy. Responsible.

About half an hour after we open, the old guy who loves Diane shows up. Same sharp suit and crooked spine. Same lost stare. Morgan says hello. The old guy seems shocked, glancing at me like he wants me to give the OK. I smile and pretend to be busy. Morgan asks his name, and I feel so stupid for not asking him before. He says William or Walter or something else, then heads over to classic fiction.

Not long after, a tall man with a baby strapped to his chest walks in. The two of them are wearing matching navy-blue bucket hats, the baby facing out. We watch the pair of them scan the shop, four eyes moving like they all belong to one two-headed creature. Both heads tilt the same way when they notice my hair.

"Morning," says Morgan, stepping out from behind the counter. "Can I help?"

"Maybe," says the man. "I'm looking for something on mindfulness, for my wife."

Morgan looks back at me. I point to the back corner.

"This way, please," he says, walking round. The man and his baby follow as another customer walks in.

It's the DJ girl from Sean's gig. Rumer. Why do I even remember her name?

You're not here.

She smiles as she walks over. I look back at Morgan with the tall man, then start to neaten up the counter.

"Nice place," she says. She's wearing a violet sweater that's at the perfectly worn-in stage.

"Thanks." I say. Miles Davis's name in my head. "Are you looking for something?"

She smiles again.

"Yeah."

"You know what it feels like?" Morgan says, biting into his panini on the sofa. "It feels like being in a sitcom."

I crunch my Monster Munch. We didn't lock the shop for lunch. It's fine with two people.

"You know what I mean?" he says.

"I guess. So you'd be the privileged guy who's never had a job before?"

"Very funny. And what about you? The kooky comic-book girl?"

He smirks. "I remember, Marcie. You and your graphic novels. I've seen *Ghost World*, you know." I laugh by accident and his smile widens.

"So what was that girl after?" he says, and my body tenses.

"What girl?"

"The one who came in before, with the funky hair. I'm always intrigued by strangers' book choices."

He's not grilling me, he's genuinely curious.

"She just . . . she wanted something on Miles Davis. We didn't have it." I slide the Post-it note with Rumer's number on it under the keyboard. "I said I'd call her if we got it in."

I swivel round and run my finger along the records.

"What if you've messed up, Morgan?" I say. "What if you've pulled the plug on your future?"

Morgan frowns. "Oh no. Is my future a bath?"

"You know what I mean. What if you regret it?"

"I do regret it."

"Yeah?"

"Yeah. Twice a day. Once when I wake up in the morning and think, what the hell did I do? And then again just before I fall asleep and I think, seriously, what the hell did I do?"

He takes another bite.

"That sounds like a mistake to me," I say.

Morgan wipes his mouth. "Maybe. But at least it'll be mine."

A shudder runs through me. "What did you say?"

Morgan looks at me. "I said at least it'll be mine. From the book?"

I feel like I'm sinking into the stool.

"Have you really not read it?" he says.

I crunch another crisp to compose myself. "No."

There's a silence. One of those two-people silences when you can feel the other person's brain trying to choose the right words.

Morgan looks at me. "Is it because it's about your mum?"

And an arrow hits my sternum. I look down and reach for another crisp, but the packet is empty. I feel like a zoo animal. A lonely panda sitting on a concrete slab, spotlight shining in my face, exposed to the glaring public. I don't know what to say.

"*Not at all, shit stick.*"

You're standing behind the sofa, looking down at him. Your left arm is in a cast and there's a scratch on your forehead.

"*Tell him no, Marcie. And say it like you mean it.*"

Morgan's still watching me, oblivious to you. I keep a straight face. "No."

I scrunch up the empty crisp packet. "When you live with the chef, the food's never as impressive."

"*Nice.*" You nod your approval. "*Now get rid of him.*"

You smile at me. I rub my fingers on my thighs and stand up. "I think we're done for the day."

Morgan looks confused. "Done? But it's only lunchtime."

"I know. Half-day to start. Ease you in."

I step out from behind the counter. Morgan looks at his half-finished sandwich. I walk to the door. "You can eat that on your way, right? I need to speak to Dad."

You're nodding. Morgan stands up. "About me?"

"*Say yes.*"

I open the door. “Yeah, it’s kind of an appraisal thing. Discuss how you did, whether you fit the shop ethos.”

“Ethos?” He picks up his jacket and walks over slowly. “But the shop doesn’t even have a name.”

I nod. “True, but we don’t get hung up on names here. We have a certain vibe we’re going for. It’s very subtle, you know? A delicate chemistry.”

I shepherd him through the door.

“Shall I come back tomorrow then?” he says.

I tap my chin. “Let me talk to Dad. We’ll let you know. I have your number, right?”

“Yeah. Listen, Marcie, I didn’t mean to—”

“Thanks, Morgan. Speak later.”

I close the door and flip the sign. He waits for a moment, then pulls his jacket on and leaves.

“That was good.”

You’re still behind the sofa. You look tired.

I lean back against the door. “Fighting yetis again?”

You move your cast behind your back. “Not exactly.”

“I’m still angry with you, Thor.”

“I know. Lock the door.”

“Why?”

"Shop's closed for the day."

"Yeah? I think the owner might have something to say about that."

You smile. "No you don't."

I lock the door.

"I don't feel much like dancing."

You shake your head. "Me either."

"What then?"

You point to the back room. "Unfinished commission. We don't have much time."

You offer me your arm. "If you'd be so kind, m'lady."

☆

You're ten.

It's summer holidays. The front door is open and you're sitting in the dip on the front step, sketchbook in your lap. Down the corridor, Coral is at the kitchen table, marking essays, Billie Holiday playing from the back-room stereo, the warm, soapy smell of laundry.

I'm sitting on next-door's silver bin. Legs crossed. Watching you draw.

"Talons of a peregrine falcon," you say, smiling as you move your pencil.

Good choice, I say, and scratch my chest.

"Your turn, Thor Baker." Your hair is in a tight knot on top of your head. You're wearing light blue dungarees over a white T-shirt. The street is quiet.

"Wings of a pteranodon," I say. You frown.

I lift my chin, proud and spread my arms. Wingspan over six metres.

You smile.

"You're smart, Thor Baker." You start on the wings.

And the body of a robot! I add. You outline the body without even looking up. I am beaming. Everything is perfect.

"I'm going to be a comic-book artist," you say. "I will draw all day."

"Sounds perfect," I say. "What about the head?"

You're already starting it. I can see a snout.

"What is it, Marcie?"

You look up at me, squinting in the sunshine. "It's a bear."

And it's the best idea I have ever heard.

☆

Watching you feels just as magical as it used to.

Your hand leads the pen over the wall like they're dancing, leaving a trail of wet, shiny black as they go. The line that you started becomes the edge of the tower block. It takes up most of the wall. The grid of windows. Leyland's shack and the aerials on the roof. The Ferris wheel.

I describe details, but you're almost ahead of me, like you're reading my mind. You layer the background with other buildings and make-believe structures. A monochrome skyline of the not real.

You finish adding the final line of an aerial and step back, pushing the top back on to the pen. The high window casts a strip of yellow on to the tops of the buildings that looks like the sharp city sky.

You sit down on the bed next to me and we both take in the wall.

I nod.

You take a deep breath. "There's more, right?"

You look at the wall to our left where the sofa used to be.

I nod again.

"Yep."

You roll you head back against your shoulders and twist your wrists.

"Good."

☆

I don't want to stop.

I wish the wall stretched out forever and I could never run out of ink.

It feels like the pen is leading me. Like there's music playing somewhere far away that only it can hear, and I'm just along for the ride.

The lamp is on and the shadows have come to life. The city feels 3D.

You describe buildings, shapes, and it's like I can see them. Windows and bricks. Scales and ladders. Weird and wonderful structures that make no sense, but perfect sense, and as I draw it feels like I'm falling forward, letting things go. Flying through time.

"It's grand but not scary," you say as I curve the lines of a path.

"Like Wayne Manor?"

"Exactly."

"But she lives in the shed?" I draw the curved arch of a main doorway.

"She doesn't like privilege."

I stop and look at you. You shrug. "She's complicated."

I start a new line. "I like the sound of her."

I hear Dad coming down the stairs. You cross your legs on the bed and look at me, letting me know you're not going anywhere. I nod, letting you know I agree.

He's got his jacket on, and shoes, and he's happy.

"Where you off to?" I say. "What time is it?"

"Don't know. Just to the garage. Holy shit! What's this?"

He steps in, checking out the walls. I look at you.

"*Fridge City*," you say, smiling.

I put the top back on my pen. "It's Fridge City."

Dad scans the pictures, drinking in details, smiling like a little boy. "It's incredible!"

A wave of embarrassment crashes over me, and I look down.

"*Get your head up, Marcie. Right now*."

So I do. And my embarrassment melts, leaving just the fledgling glow of pride.

"Thanks," I say, looking at you.

Dad steps to the wall and traces a dry line with his fingertip.

"Mars, it's so good. I love it!" He looks at me. "And who lives in Fridge City?"

You smile from the bed and wink at me.

I shrug. "All sorts."

Dad pats me on the back and squeezes my shoulder. "It makes me so happy seeing you create."

And I feel close to him. My idiot artist father.

"Double celebration then!" he says, rubbing his hands together. "Even more need for ice cream!"

"Why?"

Dad grins. "I think I finished my first chapter."

"Loads," you say, through a mouthful of Ben & Jerry's Chocolate Fudge Brownie.

I lick the back of the spoon and scoop out a fresh chunk. "But these ones are the main places you go?"

You nod, digging a claw into the tub.

Dad's upstairs with his Cookies and Cream, reading over his first new full chapter in seven years. We're on the floor, backs against the bed, looking over at eight hours' work. My hand and wrist ache. The skin on my middle finger is raw from pen pressure. And I love it.

A small shed in front of a mansion, an empty corridor, a fountain that looks like a rocket, an empty, tattered train carriage, the corner of a warehouse, the tower block and your picture of Coral's house fill the foreground of the two walls. Behind them, a backdrop collage of dragons and water slides, castles and bridges stretching away, as though I could stand up and walk right into the city. It's pretty damn good if I do say so myself.

"Fridge City."

"Yep."

"With your friends?"

"Sometimes."

Sean right now. In the kitchen. Or on the patio. Looking at Jordan. Looking at Cara.

Trying to figure it out.

"Did it work, Thor?"

You spoon a brown glacier into your mouth. "Guess we'll see."

You bang your forehead, trying to fight the brain freeze.

"Will you be in trouble for sharing all this with me?" I say.

You squeeze your eyes shut, waiting for your brain to thaw. "Probably." You hand me the spoon. "Doesn't matter though."

"Why not?"

You point at the walls. "This is your thing, Marcie. This is you."

I stare at the picture. The feeling of magic. Of purpose. "Maybe."

There are the scratching sounds of tiny claws on the hallway linoleum, then Calvin bounds into the room like she's leading a carnival procession. She goes straight for the tub. I lift it out of her reach. "Not for you, monster."

You scrape some out with a claw and offer it to her. She hesitates, then starts licking.

"You're a bad influence, Thor Baker."

You smile. "I am what you made me."

Calvin finishes cleaning your claw and starts bouncing like she's ready to go to war. I point to her scratching post. "Destroy!" She runs over to it and starts raining the pain, and I'm wishing I was a cat so bad.

"It's a big deal, right –" you point upstairs – "finishing a chapter?"

"Huge," I say, "and no flying furniture must mean he still likes it."

"Cool. You being close helps him."

I take another spoonful and feel Mum's name float into the room like a lost fairground balloon.

"Do you think I was a bit harsh with Morgan? He didn't mean anything by it."

"Who cares? It's none of his business."

You dig in the tub again.

"I can talk about her, Thor."

You eat.

"It's not like she's some kind of forbidden topic."

You shrug and eat more.

"It's weird to people," I say. "From the outside, it doesn't make sense."

Calvin stops her attack and stretches out. You hand me the tub. There's only a shallow crater of ice cream left. "Doesn't make that much sense from the inside either."

Quiet.

"When will you tell him?"

"Not yet."

I drop the spoon into the tub.

"What if it's a mistake, Thor?"

I stare at your wobbly drawing of Coral's house. I can hear you breathing.

I can hear you thinking. And you know I'm thinking the same thing.

At least it'll be mine.

TUESDAY

(1 DAY LEFT)

"He did it!"

"Car? What time is it?"

"It's late. Early. Who cares? Can you hear me OK?"

"Yeah."

"He kissed me, Mars!"

"What?"

"He kissed me! On the mouth! I kissed him! We kissed!"

"Who did?"

"What does that mean? Who do you think? Sean!"

"Sean?"

"It was perfect, Mars!"

"When?"

"Earlier. Last night. After the fire."

"Where is he?"

"He's gone to get the blanket and drinks – we're gonna watch the sun rise. You should see it. It's incredible."

"Wow."

"That's it? That's all you're going to say?"

"No, I mean it's great! What about Jordan?"

"Jordan? Did Sean call you?"

"No."

"Then how do you know . . .?"

"I don't know anything. What happened?"

"He tried it on."

"Jordan?"

"Yeah. I told you he's been weird since we got here, right? Like real forward. Like all of a sudden he fancies me."

"Did he say that?"

"He didn't say anything; that's why it was confusing. We went out on his mum's fella's boat in the afternoon – him, me, Sean, Mya, Luke and Leia – and we're just floating or whatever, and he's getting all touchy and stuff. Acting like we're three couples or something, like me and him, we're a thing. Anyway, I told him to back off. He got all arsey. Sean stepped in. They start arguing."

"On the boat?"

"Yeah. Not like, full on, but then, when we get back and we're making dinner, they start arguing again in the garden and the next thing you know they're proper going for it."

"Fighting?"

"Yeah! Luke had to break it up. It was crazy."

"Why were they fighting?"

"Because of me!"

"What?"

"Exactly! Crazy! Turns out Jordan likes me, or whatever, and Sean thought I liked him."

"Jordan?"

"Yeah, I know! Anyway, who cares? He likes me! Sean likes me! He's liked me for a while!"

"And then he kissed you?"

"No. Later. When it all calmed down. After the fire. He likes me! Can you believe it? Mars?"

"I'm here."

"Did you hear me?"

"Yeah. That's great."

"I feel like I'm dreaming! I'm on the beach right now. The light is just . . . wow! I wish you could see it. Did you get the photos?"

"What photos?"

"I WhatsApped photos. Put WhatsApp on your phone."

"OK."

"Are you all right? You sound sad."

"No. I'm just. Tired."

"I'm taking a picture of this sky right now. It's like some next-level kind of orange. We're driving back tonight."

"Right."

"Aren't you gonna say anything else? I kissed Sean, Mars. It might be a thing! Can you believe it?"

"Course I can. I always did. Listen, Car—"

"Oh, I can see him – he's coming back. I've gotta go. I'll see you tomorrow, all right? Love you. It's so perfect! Bye."

I put my phone on the floor and stare at the wall, my eyes still adjusting to the light.

Your tower block is pale and flat. Everything is quiet.

"It worked," I say.

You reach your heavy bear arm around me. I'm the little spoon.

I squeeze your paw to my chest, pressing my back against you.

"You knew it would."

I stroke your fur. Feel you breathing. "You OK?"

I close my eyes.

"I don't even know."

Dad's hunched over the typewriter like he's whispering to the keys. From behind, the string of cigarette smoke makes it look like his hair has caught fire. Burning with ideas.

"Still going good?" I say.

Dad gives a blind thumbs-up with one hand, still typing with the other.

Calvin comes skidding out of the kitchen and rubs herself against my ankles.

I scoop her up and go to the kitchen.

As I spoon dark granules on to a new filter, I picture Cara and Sean kissing. The glow of the fire dancing on their skin. His hand on her face. Her hand on his chest. And I feel a weight. A heaviness. As though gravity decided to concentrate specifically on me. Pulling me down, from inside.

Truth hurts.

The dirty dishes in the sink look like the skeleton of

an animal. Tiny smears of food on the bones. "I need to go back to the house, Dad, pick up a few things. No shop today."

I fill Calvin's bowl with dry kitten food and top up her water. "Dad?"

Dad doesn't respond.

I wash two mugs, pour black coffees, and leave one next to him on my way back to the stairs.

☆

Sun beats down on the guts of the house.

The sky is a perfect HD blue-screen, swiped with animal clouds and vapour trails.

I sit in Coral's armchair, surrounded by waist-high piles of rubble.

To my left, the stairs are now open-air. The entire outer shell is gone: no front, back or roof. Only the central wall behind me, and the perpendicular, load-bearing wall, keep the upstairs landing in place. Your bedroom door is now the highest point of the structure.

It's like somebody pulled all the petals off a

house-sized concrete flower, leaving just the chipped brick stamen.

Last night was perfect.

Watching you draw. Lying with you.

Being there.

One more day, Marcie.

One more day.

I watch a plane cut a straight line aiming this way.

How many people on board? Where are they going?

Three hundred miles per hour looks like a snail's pace from down here.

Why have I never left the city?

Truth is, I didn't want to be far, in case I was called. Like a tiny part of me always knew it would happen, through all the years.

Maybe I will now. Maybe, when the dust settles, I'll get on a plane and fly somewhere else. Somewhere new.

Reset.

Restart.

The plane keeps coming. Sure of its path.

How far will they go? What will they see?

Is it getting lower?

Her hands are by her sides, dark hood billowing behind her head.

She raises her arms like she's on a crucifix and pushes her feet out in front, treading the air to slow down, then hovers above the house across the street.

I clap. "Impressive."

Blue puts her hands in my old hoodie pockets and floats down across the street towards me, walking in the air, not breaking stride as she steps on to the thin landing strip of dusty brown carpet.

"You've been busy," she says.

"Nearly done."

"Can I sit down?"

"Course."

She holds her hand out and the rubble-covered sofa lifts up and tilts. Broken bricks and plaster tumble to the floor. She waves left, and the sofa turns in the air, under her control, then sets down next to me.

"Not a bad way to travel," I say.

She brushes dust off the sofa arm and sits close. "Beats the train."

Shards of glass dotted in the rubble twinkle like diamonds. I lean forward and pick up a chunk of pale brick.

"It used to piss me off so much, you know? Like, why would you make me and not have me fly?"

I toss the brick on to the nearest pile.

"We've all got our gifts," says Blue, crossing her legs. "My thing was always, how come we can even see each other? All these different makers, these separate minds, and yet I'm here talking to you in the same space? Nobody could ever explain that."

"I asked the same thing. Leyland told me it's because they're all connected. They don't always think they are, but they are. Shared memories. Instincts. All the stuff they don't understand about their brains. I guess it makes sense."

"Maybe. How old is he now?"

"I don't actually know. Old enough to talk in pure proverbs with a straight face."

Blue smiles. "That'll be you soon enough."

The faint sound of a siren wails somewhere back in town. The air is heavy with a sense of ending.

"It's tomorrow, right?" she says.

I nod.

"Does she know?"

I turn and look at her. "She has no idea."

"They don't realise the power they have, Thor. Any of them."

I close my eyes and feel you in my arms, your fingers stroking my paw.

"Probably better that way."

"And are you ready?"

Open my eyes. "Does it matter?"

A cloud shaped like a sausage dog floats in front of the sun.

"And has it felt different, this time?" she says.

"Yeah. Now she knows what she wants."

"And what's that?"

"Time. She wants time, for herself. For ideas. For not following plans."

"And you're helping her get it?"

"I'm helping her try."

Blue stares into her lap. "You love her, don't you?"

Your smile as you draw. Back then. Last night.

"Yeah."

Blue nods to herself. I hold out my paw.

"I'm sorry I can't be what you want, Blue."

She looks at me. "I know you are."

She takes my paw and we sit, among the rubble. Old friends who don't need to speak.

"Do you remember the oath?" she says after a while.

"Yeah."

"I thought it this morning, haven't done that for years. Just making a coffee and I realise I'm speaking the words. Funny, right?"

"It's ingrained in all of us, Blue."

"Yeah," she squeezes my paw. "Good luck, Baker."

She lets go and stands up. "Come find me when you feel like a trip out to the river. I'll buy the chicken."

The cloud passes and everything washes golden.

"You're too good for me, Princess Blue."

Blue smiles. "I know."

She floats up, until her feet are as high as

where the ceiling should be, then shoots away like a firework.

☆

It's too quiet.

Like nobody has lived here for years.

Standing in the dark hall, I breathe in memories. Dad's face, waving goodbye. Coral on her knees, hugging me tight, pinning my arms to my sides.

I stare at the stairs. Stare at the stairs. Homophone.

Hold out my hand and stroke the wall as I climb.

The bathroom door is on its side across the doorway to stop people falling.

I lean in through the frame and stare down into the kitchen. The bath, smashed table and all the rubble have been cleared out ready to start the rebuild. Like the prep before surgery.

A graft of new floorboards.

I take out my phone and hold it over the edge, the urge to drop it swelling inside me.

Just to see if it would smash.

*

My room feels smaller somehow.

I flop on to my bed and look up at my map.

Coral helping me pin it up, pointing out how misleading it was. How Britain was only a third of the area of France in real life, but on a map is made to look the same size.

"Same old imperial mindset, Mars."

Her stern face, thinking about white European colonialism.

Me nodding, thinking about *Star Wars*.

I smile to myself as I reach underneath the bed.

It's crazy that a box file feels like a safe place to keep important things. It has no real lock. No elaborate booby-trap defences. It's just a cuboid of cardboard, built to hold paper. Tracing the edge of it in my lap, I look up at my shelves.

Top two: graphic novels, comics and manga. The maroon letters of *100 Bullets*. The yellow and black of *Lady Snowblood*. Middle shelf: favourites. Books I've read multiple times. *The Outsiders*. *Marcelo in the Real World*. *The Basketball Diaries*. *Broken Soup*. Bottom two shelves: everything else. Stuff from Dad. James Baldwin. Margaret Atwood. Raymond Carver. Murakami. Jean Rhys. Some

I've read. Some I've tried to read.

How many hours? How many characters? How many worlds?

All of them ready, whenever I am.

And there.

Bottom right corner. Last one along. Thin grey spine.

Like one rotten tooth, waiting to be pulled.

The only one I've never opened.

But can't get rid of.

The house casts its shadow down the lawn.

I lean forward in the garden chair, box file between my feet, Dad's book in my hands.

The front cover is mostly empty grey space with the title at the top and, at the bottom, half a street-light bulb, the filament burned out red, and one quote:

"Striking."
– the *Independent*

The back cover shows the other half of the bulb and the corner of a flat, tarred roof.

Written in the grey sky in white:

`The real us lives in dark corners.`

Seven words, courier font.

It's not much thicker than an exercise book. The smooth matt finish and perfectly unbent edges satisfying to stroke. As a thing, an object, it's kind of gorgeous.

I stand up.

Arm back. Loaded. Ready.

And I throw.

The pages flutter briefly as the book arcs through the air. For a moment, it seems to hang. A dark, rectangular bird against the sky. Then it falls, spiralling down, and hits the grass next to the old dead tree.

Cement in my stomach. Two parts guilt. One part relief.

"Stupid books."

You're standing behind the other garden chair.

"They're so smug. Ooh, look at us, we're so clever. Too clever for you: you wouldn't understand us."

"They're not people, Thor."

"They don't do anything." You sit down. "They just sit there, waiting for you to pick them up and do all the work. Hundreds and hundreds of pages, just to get to the exact same two words. The End." Your face seems to flicker. "Gimme a rock. Or a bat. Something useful. Something solid."

"Where have you been?"

"I had to finish something, at work."

"And is it done?"

"Pretty much."

I look at you. "What's going to happen, Thor?"

"I don't know."

"But you'll be with me, right?"

"Marcie, I . . ."

Then you're gone.

Then you're back.

Like a jump in a film. A skipped frame. "Thor . . ."

You look at me. "Marcie."

And disappear.

☆

Spread out on your landing.

And I can't move.

Watching the fireflies hover above me, it feels like there's a double-decker bus on my chest.

Tell myself to stay calm. It's fine. I'm already on the floor so I can't fall. This will pass. Your face.

You'll be with me, right?

Oh, Marcie. Why don't you know?

The fade is here.

Deep breaths.

I need to be clever. Limit my time.

I reach out and touch your door. Want to get back to you.

But not now. I'm too weak.

I need to get home.

☆

I watch the empty chair, waiting for you to reappear.

What was that? Are you OK?

Look at my empty hand.

Gimme a rock. Or a bat. Something useful. Like a pen?

I reach into the box file and take out the letter from Mum.

The faded postmark. My name.

What will I say to her?

"Hungry?"

Coral's holding a brown chicken-shop bag, leaning in the patio doorway, trouser suit matching her handbag. My Coral. Respected university psychology lecturer, with a chicken-shop loyalty card.

I drop the letter on top of the box file and push it under my seat.

"Day off?" she says.

"Wanted to pick up a few things."

"Me too. They start on the ceiling tomorrow." She sits down where you were.

"Coral, listen . . ."

"Shhh. Let's not." She takes out a flame-covered, family-sized box of chicken and smiles. "I got you wings."

"It's good for you both," she says. "Quality time."

I nod. The garden is almost fully in shadow, just a thin wedge of light down near the tree.

"He's finished a first chapter."

"That's great. Maybe you're the muse this time." She smiles.

I picture Dad, hunched over the typewriter, furiously tapping like the world is about to end.

"I didn't understand all the fuss, to be honest," Coral says, shaking her head. "Maybe it's the big sister in me."

I wipe my mouth. "I've never read it."

"Good for you."

We both stare down the garden. I can just make out Dad's masterpiece in the shady grass.

"I guess it was my way of getting him back," I say.

"For what?"

"For letting her go."

"Oh, Marcie." Coral's maternal smile. "What a silly mess they made."

I look down between my feet at the letter. One line. Seven words. From a stranger.

Coral closes the lid on the box of bones. "They were so young."

I twist my napkin in my fingers.

"Is it us, in the story, Coral? Is it our lives?"

"No. Yes. In a way." She cleans between her fingers with a wet wipe. "Through the jumbled-up lens of a man who didn't get the answers he wanted, so made them up."

"So it is about her?"

"In part, yes, his version. He gave as good as he got, Mars, trust me. Those two. Man oh man. Artists . . ." She gestures, one hand moving down, the other moving up. "Two manic people only really meet when they're heading in opposite directions."

"Artists?"

A gentle breeze lifts the edges of the spare napkins. Coral stares off into a memory.

"They used to call me 'doc'. Laugh at me for studying so much while they hung out, quoting poets, smoking and listening to Led Zeppelin. Like I wasn't allowed to 'understand' Miles Davis because I was academic." She rolls her eyes. "They were so full of it, Mars."

"What if I found her, Coral? What if I knew where she was?"

The last sliver of sunlight slips behind the house, and Coral's expression turns harsh.

"She left, Marcie. He stayed."

And I feel the fight rise in me. "What? Like he deserves a medal for that? Like that's not just what he's supposed to do? He's my father, Coral."

"And she was your mother." The air turns colder. One punch each.

Whoever strikes next sets the tone. It's her. "My love, it's not a defeat to accept something you can't change. Do you understand? It's a strength." She taps the table. "The man is flawed, Marcie, in many, many ways. But he loves you, more than anything."

I nod.

"Look at me, Marcie."

I do. And her eyes are the same as that first night. Full of fire and love. "We can't blame empty space. We can only blame who we can see."

She offers her hand. I take it.

"My career was everything to me. Everything. Making a name for myself at the university, respect in the department. A woman has to work twice as hard in academia, I know you know that, and a black woman? I got to a point where having children felt like a ship that had sailed, you know? And then you came along and showed me what family is."

Her smile is shaking.

Coral Baker.

Doctor of psychology.

Surrogate mother.

Sure and strong. How much of her is in me?

"I love you, Coral." The words march out of my mouth. And she cries.

Squeezing my fingers, she cries the kind of tears a mother cries when her child leaves home. "You're going to do amazing things, Marcie Baker. You are special. Always have been."

She wipes her eyes with her free hand.

"Coral," I say.

Can you see me, Thor? Everything is happening.

"There's something I have to tell you."

☆

There's nothing as scary as feeling weak.

Slumped in my seat, riding the empty six back to Central, that's exactly what I feel. Like my body isn't fully under my control. Like somebody turned all my senses down, muffling the world.

Even the click-clack of the carriage wheels, that sounds so familiar, has taken on a different life. The steady rhythm of a turning grindstone now feels like the amplified, irregular beat of my own heart.

The fireflies are hovering in front of me again. I try to swat them, but my paws feel numb. I watch my arms moving as though they're separate from the rest of me, then my right paw passes straight through my left and a spike of cold terror shoots through me.

I shake my head and try again. This time my pads touch and I grip tightly, squeezing hard in relief.

The train pulls into Needle Park and the doors open.

I press the seat either side of me, steadying myself.

The old hunchback guy steps on. Must've clocked off early.

He sits opposite and I see him smile through the cloud of spots. I nod, moving my paws to my lap as the doors close and the train starts to move.

"How long?"

I hear the words without his mouth even moving. Did he speak?

"Yes. I did." Again, his mouth doesn't move, but his voice is in my head, old and soft like low piano keys. "I'm Warren, Thor."

How does he know my name?

He smiles and leans forward, the hump between his shoulders showing itself. I think about tomorrow, your bedroom floor, that first night.

Warren gives a serious nod. "Of course. Soon." He's reading my mind. Speaking without speaking. He can hear my thoughts. All this time?

All these years?

And suddenly I'm sinking down into my seat. Through it. My feet and legs are disappearing into the floor of the carriage, an empty cold seeping through all of me.

I reach out to Warren, filling with fear. Help.

Warren takes my paws, gripping my wrists, and his touch is the only definite thing in the world.

"It's the fade."

He lifts his chin, straining, and there's a kind of ripping sound, like cloth being torn, then his shoulders burst through his coat. Thick black stumps like horns, moving, growing. He's not a hunchback.

He has wings.

His face contorted in pain, he rolls his shoulders back and long, glossy black feathers fan out either side of his thick body, each wing more than twice the length of him.

He starts pulling, and my body lifts, sliding out of the chair like the sword from the stone. I look into his eyes and his voice is crystal clear in my head. “Home.”

Then he bursts up, dragging me with him, smashing through the roof of the train.

☆

In and out of consciousness.

Cool air and thin cloud all around me. Passing through me.

The dull beat of Warren’s wings.

I am falling forward through time.

A sense of nothingness. Of air.

Freedom.

This is what it feels like to fly.

We touch down on the roof.

The disappointment of no longer flying is beaten down by the relief that my legs and feet feel solid again. I ball my fists and bang my paws together.

"It will come in waves," says Warren, wings swaying slightly either side of him. "You should go to bed."

I take a deep breath, and nod. "Thank you."

Warren smiles. "If you can't let go, you'll never fly."

He climbs up on to the ledge, and he takes off.

Heavy black wings beating the air.

Higher and higher.

A dark shape, shrinking into the sky.

☆

Lock the shop door and breathe.

Coral's face when I told her. Shock turning into disbelief, morphing into anger, settling on concern. She didn't like it but she understands.

She wants to understand.

Calvin scampers in from the back. I bend down to meet her, the box file tucked under my arm, then Morgan steps from behind the central pillar and I scream like Janet Leigh in the *Psycho* shower scene.

Calvin spins round and darts back out.

"No! Sorry! It's just me. It's Morgan."

He's holding up one hand, the other pressing a tea towel against his head.

"Jesus, Morgan. What happened? What are you doing here?"

"I'm sorry, Marcie. I didn't know what to do."

I know it's Dad before he says anything else. He wobbles to the till stool and sits down.

I walk over and see a decent, egg-sized lump above his right eye, a small lightning bolt of red right in the centre. The tea towel has a patch of blood and there's spatters on his T-shirt.

"Holy shit! Are you OK?"

Morgan checks the tea towel, then puts it back against the bump.

"I'm all right. It's stopped bleeding now."

"Let me see."

I step behind the counter and he moves the towel again.

"Shit, Morgan. Are you dizzy? Did you throw up?"

"No. I'm fine, seriously. It was my fault."

I lean on the counter. "What did he do?"

Morgan dabs his lump with the towel. "Marcie, really, I shouldn't have intruded. He was working." I feel my blood bubbling as he pushes hair away from his face.

"I came to see you really. To say sorry, for yesterday," he says.

"There's no need."

"I wanted to. I was out of order prying. It's none of my business. But you weren't here. I knocked and rang the bell, but you didn't come, so I was just gonna go when your dad came down."

"Was he mad?"

"No. No, he was fine. Made me a coffee and everything. He said he didn't know where you'd gone. I offered to watch the shop while he carried on working."

"It was really quiet, just that old guy Warren in the suit. He stayed a while, then left. Then I hear this crash, from upstairs. Then another one. Like a table being flipped or something, and stomping, and I didn't know what to do. I mean, it's a solitary thing, right? Writing? Somebody's process is their process, especially someone as talented as he is. I mean, who am I to interfere?"

He lowers the towel. The skin of the lump has that stretched shine to it.

"But then it goes quiet and I hear something else." A concerned look fills his eyes. "I think he was crying, Marcie."

Morgan looks down guiltily, like he committed a crime just by witnessing one of Dad's swings.

"Is he upstairs?" I say.

Morgan nods. "I haven't heard anything since I came back down." He shrugs. "That was about an hour ago."

"I'm so sorry, Morgan. Do you want me to come with you to A&E?"

"No. I'm good. Honestly. Just a bit of a headache. It was a good-sized ashtray. I mean, I should've ducked really. He's a good shot, man."

He gives a weak smile. I shake my head. "He's an idiot."

"What's that?"

He's pointing at my box file. I move it behind my back. "Nothing. Just old ideas."

Morgan smiles. "They're usually the best ones."

I look towards the stairs. Johnny Cash stares at me blankly.

"Wait here," I say. "I'll be right back."

He's huddled in the corner, between the sofa and the wall.

The table is on its side again, typewriter and paper splashed on to the floor. The ashtray is near my feet in the doorway, a jagged glass planet circled by dark ash and crumpled butts.

Brown streaks of coffee have dried on the window, a dirty filter on the end of the day.

"What's wrong with you?"

Dad looks over. "Is he OK?"

"No, Dad. You threw a glass ashtray at his face."

"I didn't mean to hit him. I just threw it, and he was there."

"Oh, that's all right then."

"Mars . . ."

"I'm taking him to the hospital for an X-ray."

"I'll drive."

"No, you won't, I'm embarrassed enough already. You can give me some money for a taxi."

His head goes down. "There's cash in my jacket pocket."

I go to the coat hooks and pull out a handful of crumpled notes. Calvin walks in like she's here to dust for prints. I look round the room.

"You ever wonder whether it's worth it, Dad?"

He heaves himself up and sits on the sofa. "All the time. Sometimes I wish I could just turn it off—" he bangs his forehead with his palm – "stop myself living in here."

I take a step towards him, then remember Morgan is downstairs.

"Dad . . ."

"I deserve it, Mars." He looks at me. "I deserve it all."

And I want to hit him. I want to run over to the sofa and smack him right in his self-absorbed, tortured-author face. *Do it, Marcie*, you'd say if you were here. *Do it right now.*

I stare at him, the urge to smash something boiling inside my chest. Dad shakes his head, lost. "She wanted to leave, Mars." His eyes are filling with tears. "What could I do?"

My hands ball into fists, strangling the notes. Choking the life out of something. Anything.

"People do what they want, Dad, remember?"

I stuff the money into my jeans pocket and look down at him.

"And weak people do nothing."

Calvin miaows. I point at her. "Feed the cat."

And I leave.

☆

You're watching a young nurse shine a light into Morgan's eye.

You repeat the story you told the woman at reception, that you were chasing him, messing around, and that he hit his head on the corner of a shelf. The nurse gives Morgan a disappointed look, then tells him he has a mild concussion. No stitches are needed, but it will be tender for a few days. He gives him a cold pack and lets you go.

You accidentally step together into the revolving doors and have to shuffle slowly round, his body squeezed against yours.

You get into one of the black cabs waiting near the ambulance bays. The taxi driver thinks you're a couple. You both look out of your own window, embarrassed. Morgan tells him you are old friends, and it feels nice. The driver looks at Morgan and makes a distasteful joke about domestic violence. Neither of you laugh.

Your phone beeps. It's a text from Cara saying they're halfway home, she has had the best day ever with Sean and that she has news.

You wonder what you will say to her when you see her tomorrow. You think of what you said to Coral, but that was different.

This is Cara. The girl with the plan.

Morgan asks you if you're OK.

You stare out at the dark dual carriageway. The snake of regular street lights curving away into the night.

You feel the crackle in your stomach. And tell him everything.

I don't write, like Dad.

I draw.

I scratch out what I see in my head. Press carbon on to paper. It makes more sense.

Words feel too small. Too narrow.

But sometimes I like to try.

I think I'm five.

Sitting against the inside railing of the park bandstand, I'm watching her dance in the middle. She spins and dips like only dancers can, twisting and falling; her body moves like a leaf caught in a breeze, her long brown hair trailing and rippling like a gymnast's ribbon.

It's late afternoon and there's nobody else around. The shadows of the bandstand pillars look like dark trees on the floor. I want to tell her it looks like she's dancing through a forest, that it's like watching a fairy tale, but her eyes are closed and I'm scared to break the moment.

I'm wondering what music she can hear in her head to move this way.

I'm wondering why I can't hear it.

I want to dance too. Follow her into the forest.

But I don't know the way.

WEDNESDAY

(LAST DAY)

THOR BAKER:
FADE COUNSELLING SESSION 7

8AM

I got you still water.

Yeah, thanks.

Do you want some?

Not really. Sorry.

No problem. So, here we are.

Yep.

How're you feeling?

I'm OK, I think. Yesterday was a bit intense.

Some weakness?

That might be an understatement.

I remember I fell into the road.

Because of the fade?

Yeah. At rush hour. I was waiting at the crossing, and my legs just gave way. I fell forward. Thought I was going to drop right through the concrete.

What happened?

I kind of stopped myself with my hands, somehow, kept myself on all fours, then I look up and there's this bus coming right for me.

And you couldn't move?

No. My legs wouldn't respond, and the bus is coming. I remember the driver's eyes – he was this frog, with these big bug eyes – the fear in them, knowing he couldn't stop. I put my hands up, like that was going to make a difference.

Then what?

Then the bus passed right through me. Or more like we passed through each other. I remember seeing the feet of the people sitting on it, flying past me, going wherever they were going. Like a flashing second of shoes and shopping bags, and then I was out the other side.

How did you get out of the road?

I don't know. I came to and I was lying on the floor in the noodle bar, strangers leaning over me.

Man.

Yeah. It must be happening all the time, right? I mean, people hitting ten years, the fade. Weird that I've never seen it, with everyone in the city, you know?

We don't always see what we're not looking for. The things we don't want to face.

The truth.

Now who sounds lame?

Just practising.

Nice. So do you have a last-day plan?

I'm not sure.

But you're going to cross?

Yeah. Just for a goodbye. I mean, not that she'll even know.

And then the house will be finished?

Just the door left really. When I cross back, I'll smash it and stay on site for a while, let the fade wipe me out somewhere relatively safe.

Good idea. Just be careful. The pull will be strongest in the last moments.

So are we done?

I guess so. Unless you have any questions for me?

Not really. It's pretty straightforward. One more day with her, then get on that train.

That's right. The rest of your life is waiting.

Whoopee.

You'll be fine, Thor. Just fine.

Yeah. Just fine.

★

"When did you do it?" says Cara, through a mouthful of pancake.

She's sitting up on their kitchen counter, sun-kissed shoulders glowing next to her snug white vest.

I touch my hair. "Last week. Just felt like doing something."

I scrape a line in the puddle of syrup on my empty plate and lick my fingertip.

"I love it! It's so . . . blue!"

"Yep. You can stop staring now."

She points at my plate. "You want more? Dad made a stack."

"I'm good, thanks. Is Morgan here?"

It doesn't feel like anyone else is home.

"God knows where he is. He grunted at me on his way out earlier. No 'how was your trip?' or 'welcome back'. He's such a moody shit. And he was in a fight."

"What? Who with?"

"Dunno, but he's got a proper bruise on his face."

Morgan in the taxi, holding the cool pack to his head, listening as I told him.

His smile when I finished.

"Anyway, forget Morgan, Mars. Me and Sean!" She drums the counter with her fists. "Can you believe it?"

I scrape another line in my syrup to make a T. "It's great."

"I can't believe it! All this time, and he liked me. Crazy! I'm going to his tonight, to meet his nan. You have to help me, give me tips. I want her to like me, Mars."

I picture her on Sean's lap, eyes closed in laughter in one of those four-frame strips from a photo booth.

"Leona's lovely, Car. And she'll love you."

"You think?"

She clicks the kettle on next to her. I've seen her excited thousands of times, but I'm not sure I've seen her this happy. "What's not to like?" I say. "Pretty girl, career plan, off to university. You're a grandma's dream."

She laughs and nerves bubble in my stomach.

"*Tell her*."

You're next to their huge fridge, leaning on the wall. You smile at me. "*It's time, Marcie*."

"Car."

Cara jumps down off the counter and starts making another coffee.

"I didn't tell you the best bit yet," she says, as I watch her back. The clasp of her bra like a tiny square vertebra.

"Car, listen—"

She spins round, grinning like she just won a game show. "He's coming!"

"What?"

"Sean. He's coming with us, to Leeds!"

I look at you. You shrug.

"What do you mean?"

The spoon is in her hand like a wand. "We talked about it. He's going to look into clearing. Find a course."

"A course in what?"

"I don't know. Music, or sound engineering or something else, something he's into. How cool is that?"

You fold your arms. "*Guess it worked even better than you thought*."

Cara looks towards the fridge, then at me. "So? Say something, Mars."

I stare at my plate.

"Cool."

She sips her coffee. "How many times do you have to kiss to be a girlfriend? Am I a girlfriend? Girl friend." She laughs again. "It's gonna be so good, Mars. The three of us, out on our own."

"*Tell her*."

I look up.

"I'm not coming."

"What?"

"I'm not coming to Leeds."

She thinks I'm joking. "Yes you are. Course you are. We got in, remember?"

You nod again.

"I won't get the grades, Car."

Cara rolls her eyes. "Oh, Mars. I'm nervous too, but we'll be fine. We did the work. We studied. Trust me. We'll get what we need and we'll be gone. Just like we planned."

Shake my head.

"I won't."

She sees that I'm serious.

"Marcie, what did you do?"

TWO WEEKS AGO. LAST EXAM . . .

The clock ticks.

Ten minutes in

and my page is still empty.

All around me, a gym full of people sit in rows, heads bobbing like a gridded flock of feeding birds, speed-scrawling answers to questions we've spent months preparing for.

Every few breaths, a head will pop up, like it heard something. The distant call of that great idea. That one quote that could turn forty UCAS points into forty-eight.

This is it.

I know what I'm supposed to do. And I know what I want to do.

Last chance.

My pen tip scratches the blank paper.

Like a claw.

And then I feel you.

For the first time in years. Watching me. Knowing my thoughts.

I look up.

Across the room.

And there you are. Smiling. *Punisher* T-shirt. Older. Stronger.

I look at my empty paper. Look at you. "*Do it,*" you say.

So I draw.

It's a bookshop. Walls of shelves filled with hundreds of spines. Rows and rows of vertical stitches, each one a door to a story. A world.

The ceiling is low. Two old strip lights and peeling paint.

There are four display tables. Each one holds small towers of books that look like buildings.

That are buildings. Scale-model tower blocks and skyscrapers. Rollercoasters and castles. Miniature imaginary cities.

There is a small curved counter. With a till. And a chair.

On the chair sits a girl. Sketchbook on her lap. Pencil in hand. Hair like black fire. A smile on her face.

Musical notes dance out of the speakers behind her. A procession of black stick figures.

And to the right, half hidden behind the central supporting pillar, there is a boy.

Tall and strong. A hero's face. Arms of a bear.

Underneath the picture:

This is not a cry for help.

This is not an irrational lashing-out, or a cover-up for not doing the revision. I did the work.

This is a choice.

I know what I want, and what I want doesn't fit with other people's plans.

I could go along with things. Carry on riding in someone else's carriage and be fine.

But I don't want fine.

I want me.

I want space. And time.

To think.

And find.

Time to breathe.

Maybe I'm stupid.

Maybe I've created this feeling to try and cover up my fear. My dad says the mind can make up anything to help the body feel better about a mistake.

And maybe that's what I'm doing.

Making a big mistake.

Maybe.

But at least it'll be mine.

"You're joking, right?" Cara says.

But she knows I'm not.

"Mars, I don't understand."

"I'd like you to."

I look at you, smiling near the fridge. "*I'll see you back at the shop*," you say, and disappear.

"Car, look—"

"No, Marcie, you look. That is the dumbest thing I've ever heard in my life! Who does that? Who draws a picture on an exam paper instead of answering the question?"

"I guess I do."

Cara frowns. "No!"

"Car, I've been trying to tell you, I have, it's just—"

"You idiot! This messes everything up! We had a plan!"

"No. You did. You had the plan."

She starts pacing. "I don't believe this. What's Coral gonna say? Does she know?"

I nod.

"What? And she's cool with it? She's cool with you throwing your life away?"

"I'm not throwing my life away, Cara."

"No? So what are you doing? Explain to me exactly what it is that you're doing, Marcie."

"I'm taking some time."

"For what?"

"For me."

She stops pacing and looks round the kitchen, like she's searching for some killer point that will beat me. "What do you need time for?"

"Everything. Nothing. I just . . . it's what feels right, when I listen to myself."

I can feel the tears building as I watch the most determined person I know process this bombshell. The cinema in her head running through her pre-planned flicker book of next year, I watch her face twitch like a faulty robot.

"Car, say something. Please."

"But I need you, Mars," she says, finally. "You're my thingy. You're my rock."

I stare at the T in my maple syrup.

"I'm sorry, Car. Maybe it's time to fly."

We look at each other. Cara and Marcie. Lois Lane and Jubilee. Thrown together for some hybrid story arc.

Nothing in between us but the truth.

Cara's face screws up in disgust. "Time to fly?"

"Yeah, sorry, don't know where that came from."

"Man."

She mimes throwing up. And we laugh, relief flooding through me.

"It's the right thing for me," I say.

Cara sighs and sits down. "Sean's gonna be gutted."

"No he won't. Not with you." I hold out my hand across the table. "You'll be great together, Car."

She lays her perfect hand on top of mine and smiles.

"I get it, Mars."

"Yeah?"

"I think so." She squeezes my hand. "Maybe you just need a year out."

"Maybe."

She lets go of my hand. "You have to come up, OK? Lots!"

"Are you kidding? Watching a super journalist in her element? I'll be up all the time."

She wipes her cheeks. "What will you do?"

"I don't know. Stuff. Nothing. Read. Help with the shop. Draw."

Cara's face lights up.

"Yes! You'll be my free-spirited artist friend!"

And, as she runs into her pitch for the amended movie of our lives, I can feel in my bones that I've done the right thing.

☆

I walk down the open stairs.

Feel OK. My legs work. My arms and chest, all solid.

Maybe I'm past the worst of it?

The site looks like the set of a play about the Blitz. Mounds of rubble surround the untouched sofa and armchair.

You told her, Marcie.

You did it.

Just Dad left.

I move the two breeze blocks at the bottom of the pile nearest the armchair and take out my bag. The typewriter and box file look strange in this different setting. Everything that connects me to you has to be here for the fade.

I pour myself a coffee from Blue's flask, put the typewriter on my lap and load a fresh sheet of paper into the roll.

And I feel OK.

More than OK.

As I sip my coffee and breathe, I feel proud.

☆

You're in Cara's car.

You stare out of the passenger window as she drives you back to the shop.

You feel a strange kind of emptiness. Not the empty of something missing, more the clarity of nothing in the way. A blank page. Uncertain.

And full of possibilities.

Part of you wants to tell her what you didn't mention back at hers.

```
The letter.
Your mum.
But you don't.
That's just between you and Dad. And her.
If you find her.
```

☆

The shop is just like I left it, dark and empty.

Dad probably hasn't even ventured downstairs today and Morgan will be staying away for the foreseeable future. If Dad hadn't bought this place outright, we'd have gone under months ago. The minuscule level of business we do, if the police were surveilling the place, they'd probably believe it was some kind of front for gangsters.

I do my best cat-whisperer call, rubbing my fingertips together and making a sound like a leaking balloon. No sign or sound of Calvin. Maybe she's asleep upstairs.

Deep breath of quiet shop.

I did it.

I told her. And it's OK.

It's better than OK.

I put on some Nina Simone and sit at the till. Old music suits me more.

Nobody ever knows what's coming. People plan so that they have something to see when they look through the window of their futures, but anything can happen, no matter your plan.

I'm good with not knowing. Right now, not knowing fits.

Closing my eyes, I fill my lungs.

For the first time in forever, I feel light.

"Feeling good?"

You're sunk in the sofa, arms out either side like a mob boss.

"Yeah. I am."

"Are you going to tell Dad?"

"He's not here."

"Where do you think he's gone?"

"No idea but he took Calvin with him."

"Maybe he went to get her a collar? One of those little bells?"

"Or maybe he's in the supermarket right now, holding her up next to the cat-food packets, checking which is the right one to buy."

"Also possible."

We laugh.

"He's not going to like it, Thor."

You nod. "I know. But it's not about him, is it? It's about you."

My sketchbook is on the counter. I don't remember putting it there. I wouldn't put it there.

"You didn't."

Your smile.

"What do you want, Thor?"

"I want you to draw me, Marcie. Will you draw me, please?"

There's an special intimacy in drawing someone.

Marking your page, it's almost as though they're watching you touch them.

Each line a fingertip, traced on their skin. Knowing them. Being allowed to.

Two hours go by, and I fill pages with you. The curve of your shoulder. The cords in your neck.

The door locked, we don't speak.

When my pencil grows blunt, I fetch another and keep drawing.

The light fades outside.

And it is perfect.

Just like the beginning.

"We could just do this," I say, as I finish shading your paw.

There is a sadness in your smile. "That would be good."

You cross your legs on the sofa, elbows on knees, looking at me.

"It's OK to feel nervous," you say. "The nerves might be the only way you really know."

You are on my paper. And you are here with me.

"When did you get wise, Thor Baker?"

You fold your arms. "I'll never be wise. Just seems to me that nobody really knows anything for more than a moment. Not for sure."

"Nobody?"

Another smile.

"Nobody real."

I stroke your image on my page. "What if she doesn't want to know me, Thor? What if I manage to track her down, knock on her door, and she just shakes her head and gets on with her life?"

"Then you get on with yours." You stand up and step forward, a determined look on your face.

"Happiness can exist only in acceptance, Marcie."

You are beautiful, Thor Baker. My greatest thing.

There's a knock on the glass. Somebody peeking in through the crack next to the blind.

It's Sean.

I look at you, waiting for you to disappear.

You look at me.

And smile.

•

"Yo! Can I touch it?"

I slap his hand away before he reaches my hair and we laugh at our in-joke. Everybody always wants to touch an Afro.

"You look great, Mars."

I dodge his eyes. "Shut up."

"Sick!" He's walking over to the counter. To my sketchbook. Still open. Full of you.

I swoop past him and close it.

"That looked so good! Is it new?"

I push my sketchbook behind the computer. "No. It's nothing. Shut up."

Sean grins.

"I knew it, Mars. You don't just stop drawing. Not when you're that good. Is that what you're gonna do with yourself?"

I look at you on the sofa, watching Sean, remembering the fire.

"So will you do like a foundation course or whatever?" Sean says, face turning serious. "I spoke to Cara."

I sit behind the till. "You did a bit more than speak, Casanova."

"Mars, listen . . ."

"It's good. You did good. She's so happy."

"I'm sorry."

Your eyes don't leave him. It wasn't your fault, Thor.

"Why did you tell me she liked Jordan?" Sean says, picking up one of my pencils.

I look at you.

"I know you," I say. "We might not hang out all that much any more, but I still know you."

"You knew I liked her?"

Your eyes are closed.

"Sometimes people need a little push," I say.

Sean steps closer. "So you knew why I never said anything then?" I look down.

"I know you too, Marcie Baker," he says, and I feel the blood rushing to my face.

"I just helped you both get what you want," I say, tapping the computer keys for something to do.

"And what about what you want?" says Sean. "I see how you look at her, Mars."

You stand up, ready to defend me, but I've got this.

"I was just watching. She's into you, Sean. She always was. I'm fine. I'm not ready for any of that right now."

"Any of what?"

"I don't know. Love."

You walk over. Sean puts my pencil down.

"Marcie . . ."

"Sean. It's cool. Seriously. It's what I want. I'm going to do things just for me for a bit, you know?"

You are close enough to touch him. "*Tell him I'm sorry, Marcie. Please.*"

I see fire.

I see blood.

I see flashing lights.

"I'm sorry," I say.

Sean looks confused.

I point at his chest. He touches it.

"Every warrior needs a good scar, eh?" he says, with a smile. You smile too.

"*Thank you.*"

Sean strokes the back of his head. "I really like her, Mars."

"*I have to go, Marcie.*"

I look at you, then at him.

"I know you do."

"*Goodbye.*"

And you're gone.

The shop feels slightly colder. Like someone left a door open.

"Did you really just draw a picture on the exam paper?"

The empty sofa. The space where you were.

"Yep."

"That's so badass, Mars! And you're still pretending you're not an artist?"

I put my pencils in the mug and shrug.

"Let's see."

☆

My shadow on the landing.

It's almost sunset and the air is cool.

What is this feeling?

Part sadness, part relief.

Last chapter, heart released.

Stare at your door.

That was right. No big goodbye.

No melodramatic farewell scene.

Just you. Feeling strong. Getting on the train, of the rest of your life.

I helped, Marcie, didn't I?

Thor Baker helped this time.

Now it's done.

And I have to finish my job.

☆

He's sipping a Ribena.

Shirt open. Dots of blackberry on his white vest.

And he's got Calvin on a lead.

It's one of those telescopic ones attached to a little body harness that lets your dog wander a distance from you.

"What the hell, Dad?"

His carton gargles as he sucks the last drops through his straw.

"We went for a walk."

"You don't walk a cat."

"Why not?"

"Because it's not a dog."

"So what?" He squats and unhooks Calvin, who scampers over to me. "I used to see a guy walking a ferret every morning, back near the old house."

I scoop Calvin up next to me on the sofa and console her with strokes. "Don't worry, little one, it's over now. The crazy man won't make you pretend to be a dog again, I promise."

Dad stands up and runs his hand through his hair. "She's fine. She doesn't abide by species stereotypes. She's a freethinker."

"She's a victim," I say.

Dad looks at the sofa and shifted tables. "Nice set-up."

"Can we talk, Dad?"

"Course. Later though. I need your help."

"With what?"

"Clear-out."

"Cleaning? Dad, it's getting dark. I'm hungry. Can't it wait until tomorrow?"

"No. We can get a takeaway. It'll work better at night. More dramatic." He points at Calvin. "We'll have to keep her out of the way of course."

I scratch between Calvin's shoulder blades and she purrs like a little motor.

"Out of the way of what?"

Dad looks at me like he's already told me twenty-five times.

"The fire."

☆

I hold your door on my lap like a surfboard.

Everything is rubble. Everything is dust.

The exposed brick and steel supports of the houses either side.

What was your house is now a gap in the smile of the street.

It's done.

Just me, sitting with a rectangle of wood on the broken pile where the stairs used to be.

I stroke the smooth edge of it.

I'm good at my job.

More than good.

Nobody destroys unwanted things better than me.

I'm not crying.

It's the dust. The fine powder of crushed bricks making my eyes water.

Not tears.

We live for you, we are the made.

I stand up.

And hold your door over my head.

☆

He wasn't joking when he said clear-out.

The stuff just keeps coming. We run a production line between upstairs and the little back yard. Old clothes, books, papers, a broken chest of drawers, all get thrown into the big silver wheelie bin in the little backyard.

It's dark now, and the street light from the other side of the shop gives everything that film noir feel. Across the alleyway, the tall dark tree peers down at us as we add to the pile.

Calvin's tiny silhouette miaows through the frosted glass door to the shop each time I walk back to the stairs, my empty stomach growling in reply.

Last confession. Hardest one. Dad won't give me grief about uni, might even be excited, but going to find Mum, that might be a little bit more of an issue. With every trip inside to fetch another load of fire fodder, I practise a different set of words to lay it out, speaking them under my breath, and every single version I come up with feels awful.

"Nearly done," he says, carrying two empty wooden drawers crab-style past me through the back door.

"You're going to be sleeping in an empty room," I say, wiping my brow, feeling a trickle of sweat run down the ridge of my back.

Dad tosses the drawers into the bin. The jagged top edge of the rubbish looks like his hair.

"Clear room, clear head," he says, smiling, a sheen of sweat on his prominent collarbones.

"Why don't you go get us chicken and I'll find the lighter fluid."

"I want to talk to you, Dad."

"Not on an empty stomach, Mars. I won't be able to concentrate."

He rubs at the dark Ribena dots on his vest. "Get one of those big family buckets, will you? I'm starving."

☆

The lift feels the same.

That's the way, right?

You can make all the huge, world-shattering decisions you like, but the routine minutiae of your day really don't give a shit.

Nineteen lights up above the doors.

The familiar squeak as the brakes squeeze the lift cable and I feel the weight in my stomach rise up into my chest.

Knock the dust from my arms.

See your bedroom door in pieces at my feet.

Scooping them up.

Laying them on top of the rubble like chocolate sprinkles.

An ice-cream sundae of the past. It's done. I'm done.

`The lift doors open.`

`Pale walls and charcoal doors.`

`Same old grey.`

`This is me now. On the train with all the others.`

`Stare at the numbers. Floors. Days. Weeks. Years.`

`And push the button for the roof.`

☆

Fire is amazing.

Fire at night is even better.

Fire at night with a bucket of chicken and a cold Pepsi just might be heaven.

There's something about the flickering flames that seems to talk to the dark. Whispering dangerous secrets into the air.

We are a caveman and his blue-haired daughter, sitting on a fold-up camp chair and the back step, enjoying our takeaway hunt.

The pop and crack of expanding wood. The smell of carbon coming home.

I sip my drink and watch tiny sparks float up and die in the dark.

"I'm not going to uni, Dad."

Dad doesn't say anything. Chewing a drumstick, staring at the fire, his head is probably full of his new story. What difference does it make if his daughter shuns academia?

"Dad?"

"I know," he says. "Coral rang me."

"Oh."

There's a hiss from inside the bin as something synthetic finally succumbs to the heat.

"What did she say?"

Dad throws his bone into the fire. "She said you seemed sure."

I pull my hood on to my head and cross my legs.

"And what did you say?"

"I said OK."

He bites into a crispy thigh, and, even though I expected it, his indifference grates. Like my life choices are minuscule next to all the weighty story shit that's churning in his head.

"That's it?"

Dad chews and nods. "Yep."

"I'm passing up my degree, Dad. Opting out of further education. Don't you even have an opinion?"

Dad licks his fingertips. "What would I say, Mars? That you're making a mistake? That you're derailing your life?"

"I don't know. Something."

He wipes his mouth. "You're making a huge mistake, Mars. Completely derailing your life."

The urge to slap him sits up in my gut.

"Well, it's good to know my future's important to you."

Dad screws up his napkin and throws it into the fire.

"Coral thinks you're wasting talent. She says you would fly in a university environment."

"I'm not talking about Coral! What do you think?"

He stares intently at fire.

"I think you have to trust yourself. If not going feels right then it probably is. Only you know, Mars."

"That's not an opinion."

"Who cares about the opinion of an old man?"

"I care! I'm asking you, just for once, to please stop with the passive Yoda bullshit and act like a normal parent. Tell me what to do. Tell me I'm being stupid. That I'm throwing away the best years of my life! I don't know. Just give a shit!"

My heart is thumping.

"Do I have to fight you to give a shit?" he says. "Is that how it works? Is that what proves it?"

My hands are in fists. "At least then I'd know."

He looks at me, anger in his eyes. "You sound like your mum."

That crackle in my stomach.

"And you sound like someone who's easy to leave."

His expression flickers, a millisecond glitch where I see him gutted, staring at the door she walked out of. Then his eyes glaze over, and he turns back to the fire.

Default defensive Dad.

But I'm not having it.

Not this time.

"I'm going to find her," I say, staring at the back of his head.

He watches the flames. "She doesn't want to be found, Mars."

"No? Guess I'll ask her myself. Madrid 28070."

He doesn't turn round. Maybe he forgot about the letter.

"That doesn't mean anything," he says.

"It's a postcode, Dad. If I have that, and her name, I can find her."

Dad nods to himself, leaning forward on his knees.

"Did you hear me, Karl? I can find my mum."

The flames.

The dark.

My plan.

"No," he says, turning to me in what seems like slow motion.

"Remember, Marcie. Whatever happens, just be you."

And I feel a wrecking ball hit my chest.

"What did you say?"

Dad shifts his chair so he's facing me. My name. Handwritten.

"It was a mistake, Mars. Misguided. I just . . ." He trails off in a thought.

I feel faint. "Dad?"

He smiles, weakly. "I wanted you to have something, from her, you know? A full stop. She should have left something."

My chest is cracked glass. My head shaking.

"No."

Dad holds out his hand. "I just wanted to help."

"But Madrid 28070. She's there. Somewhere."

Dad shakes his head. "It was the book. Spanish launch.

They flew me over. I was talking to this woman, about you. I was telling her all about my amazing daughter, how you'd been through a lot, and how I wanted to be better, more present, now that I'd signed the deal and had some cash, and the idea just . . . came. I posted it the next morning. In time for your birthday."

His hand is there, waiting in the space between us.

But I am crumbling.

I am sliding off the step. It wasn't her. All this time. Not her words. Not a message. A lifeline.

Nothing.

She doesn't want to be found.

It was him.

"You."

The word bursts out of the trapdoor in my gut, climbs up my throat and jumps out at him.

"You."

"Marcie, please . . ."

But nothing matters. I'm already up.

Flying at him like a fucking bear.

☆

I can hear drums.

He's leaning on the edge, smoking as he watches the city.

I see the appeal, I really do. Night air all around you, the freedom of having nothing over your head but sky.

Maybe I could move, find a roof of my own.

"Good to see you with clothes on," I say, walking over and leaning next to him.

Leyland smokes calmly. "Time and a place, my young friend."

I look over the edge. Down on the street, some kind of procession is happening. One of those giant fire-coloured Chinese dragons ripples along followed by a solitary float holding a lone drummer.

"This place never stops," says Leyland with a smile.

"How you doing?" I say.

"You didn't come up here to enquire about my well-being, Thor."

He taps ash into the air. "You came to tell me your news."

The glowing end of his cigarette is one firefly,

hovering under his control. I point at it. “Can I get one of those?”

Leyland narrows his eyes.

I show him that I can pinch my first two claws together with an effort, and he taps out a cigarette for me. I watch the light flicker in the smooth silver of his lighter.

“Experimenting with a new persona?” he says, tucking it back into his pocket.

I inhale and hold the smoke in my throat, immediately regretting it, and shake my head.

“Just feels right tonight.”

“I see,” says Leyland, tapping the ledge. “So you’re done?”

I nod. “As of right now.”

He smiles. “Hallelujah.”

I squeeze the filter between my claws and it tears. The lit end falls, bounces on the ledge and drops over the side of the roof.

We both lean over and watch the tiny orange dot float down and out of sight.

“Shit.”

Leyland coughs out a small laugh. “Know thyself,

Thor Baker. The man with a bear's paws shall not a fiddler be." He flicks his cigarette back over his head and spreads his arms wide. "Welcome to the rest of your days."

Two car horns go back and forth down on the street. Leyland looks up to the dark sky. "This town needs an enema!"

He does a single twirl, full of tired mockery.

I drop my torn filter by my feet.

"Are you happy, Leyland?"

Leyland drops his arms as though his director just called cut.

"My dear boy, Happiness can exist only——"

"——in acceptance." I finish his sentence and look down again. "And that's what we've done, right? Accepted it? The fade?"

Leyland pulls a psychotic Joker smile. "Look! Gaze upon my happiness! As I shuffle from here to there with the rest of the cattle tapestry!"

There's trouble in his eyes.

"Are you OK?" I say.

He starts to climb up on to the ledge.

"Leyland, careful . . ."

He's laughing to himself as he kneels on the edge, his head swaying as he speaks. "*Let us listen, make us feel. Or send us off, from all the real.*"

"OK, Leyland. Come down now, yeah? Enough."

He looks at me.

"A mind can't exist in two worlds, Thor."

"Leyland, please, you're scaring me. Get down. We'll go have a drink."

I try to grab his arm, but he throws me off. His dark eyes are shining, his hair dancing in the breeze. "But wouldn't it be worth it?"

"Wouldn't what be worth it?"

"Five more minutes." He stands up. "To kiss all of this goodbye."

"Leyland . . ."

"Either or. Neither nor."

He looks down at me. "Pain is just fear leaving the body."

He holds out his arms and turns his back on the city.

"The real us lives in dark corners, Thor."

"Leyland, please! You're not making sense. Why are you doing this?"

He smiles. "Just playing my part."

Then he steps backwards and drops off the edge.

"No!"

I dive forward, holding on to the ledge, just in time to see him falling, face up, smiling like a little boy.

☆

Clawing.

Swiping at his face.

Trying to hurt him.

Scratch his eyes out.

His hands are up. Defending himself.

A few blows get through. The knife of pain in my wrist as I connect.

He falls back. I fall on top of him.

Screaming.

The heat of the fire on my side. Inside me.

A lie.

An idea built on nothing.

"Sorry."

The word slips out of his mouth so easily.

I stop.

Panting.

Salt on my lips.

Heat in my fists.

"I'm so sorry, Mars."

The guilt in his eyes. Pleading.

No.

Not enough.

Up and off him.

"Marcie?"

I don't listen.

As I run to the shop.

☆

I slump. Back against the ledge.

Head in my paws. He's gone. Smiling.

Everything muddy. The real us lives in dark corners.

Everything riddles. Stupid words. I don't understand. It feels like I'm wearing someone else's skin. A stranger. Outside of myself.

Sirens, somewhere across town. Coming for his body.

Whatever's left.

I close my eyes. To hide. To escape.

And somehow

I see you.

☆

You're tearing books from the shelves.

Wrenching them off in twos, threes, flinging them to the floor, moving on to the next, grunting like an animal.

I know this feeling.

I know it well.

Smash.

Break.

Destroy.

You charge a table full of books and they topple like cards. Pools of novels on the dark shop floor. And still you go. Ripping more and more out of their wooden bunk beds, trying to smash them like priceless vases.

Your dad is in the open doorway. Not trying to stop you. Just watching.

He wipes blood from his lip and breathes heavily.

You clear another shelf and fall to your knees, exhausted.

He says your name.

Again.

That he understands. You have to believe that.

You look at him. Backlit by the fire along the corridor.

You see the slump in his shoulders. Years bent over a typewriter.

The frame of an author.

And you stand up.

He holds out his hands as you walk to him, but you push him aside and head for the stairs.

☆

"No, Marcie!"

Open my eyes.

Feel it.

Sinking down through my spine.

Regret. Mine from back then. Yours to come.

No.

I can help.

You need me to.

But I have to be there.

☆

The pages are still next to the typewriter.

His first new chapter in years. The typed letters blurred through my tears.

This will hurt him.

This will cut.

I grab them and run back to the stairs.

He's at the bottom, waiting for me.

"Mars . . ." He sees the pages in my hand. "No!"

But I've got momentum from the stairs. I charge him and he falls back, hitting the wall and sliding down, and I'm outside, at the fire, staring into the flames.

☆

Running.

Stupid legs aren't fast enough.

Why can't I fly?

What's the point in an imaginary friend who can't fly?

Reach the park. Cut through. Shadows and dark corners.

Legs burning.

Lungs stretched like balloons.

Too slow. Need to be faster.

Hear the drums.

Close my eyes and see you. Standing by the fire. Pages in your hand.

No, Marcie.

I'm coming.

I'm coming.

☆

"Marcie, please!" He's struggling to stand, leaning in the doorway. "Don't . . ."

I hold the pages out. "This is what matters to you, isn't it?"

The cold air chills my sweat, my T-shirt stuck to my back.

"Isn't it!"

Dad coughs. "Marcie. I was wrong." He eases himself

down the wall and slumps on to the back step. "I wanted to do something. To help. But I didn't think past myself."

The white pages glow in my hand.

All his energy. His wrestles with ideas. The breakdowns. The tantrums.

All for some crooked black footprints on stupid paper.

"You are what matters. My special girl."

I hear his words but I don't believe them.

I want to do it.

I want to drop these pages in and watch them turn black. Demolish his ideas.

For letting her go.

For being so weak.

If you were here, you'd tell me to.

You'd help me do it.

Where are you, Thor Baker?

I need you now.

☆

My legs are jelly.

Can hardly breathe.

Leaning on my knees, I stare at the rubble. I'm here.

I'm here, Marcie. But you have to call.

Call me now.

"Don't do it."

The little cat is on top of next-door's bin. There's no one else around.

"Did you just . . .?"

"It's too late. The door is gone." It's a little girl's voice, six or seven maybe. We both look at the broken pieces of the house. My lungs feel like they're full of needles.

"She can still call. If I'm here."

I step forward. The cat raises a paw. "You have to let go. A mind can't exist in two worlds. If you cross now, you won't exist anywhere."

I see the spots. Dots of light hovering around her head.

"You don't understand. I can help. I know what to do."

The cat looks at me, pleading. "But what about you?"

My legs are going. Head fuzzy. I force myself to stand up straight.

"It's not about me."

☆

My hand won't move.

I want to throw his pages on to the fire. Burn his work to nothing. For all of it.

Why can't I?

"Do it, Mars."

Dad is hunched over on the step. He points at the fire. "I deserve it."

And he does.

For giving me hope. A tiny pebble of it, thrown into my lap, that wasn't even real.

His stupid book. Mining our life for a story. A wad of stupid, worthless words. Gimme a rock. Or a bat. Something that does something. Something useful. "It's your fault, Karl."

I turn back to the fire and go to throw them in.

"*Don't!*"

You're on the other side, staring at me through the flames.

"*Don't do it, Marcie.*"

What?

"*Put them down.*"

No.

"*You don't want to do it.*"

Yes I do.

"*No. It's not his fault.*"

What are you saying? You're supposed to be on my side. You're supposed to help me. That's why you're here.

"*I am. This time.*"

I want to hurt him. I want him to lose what matters.

"*He already has.*"

You look past me to Dad, arms cradling his chest, head against the wall.

"*He lost what matters before you did, but he stayed.*"

I look at the pages in my hand.

`Chapter 1 (rough)`

~~`Forgetting Ghosts.`~~

Don't do this, Thor. Not you.

"*You know the truth, Marcie. I know you do.*"

The fire between us. The fire in me.

"*It was her. She left. Her choice.*"

But he could've stopped her. He could've made her stay.

"People do what they want. And he stayed. He's not perfect. Not even close. But he's here."

I look at Dad.

His tentative smile. Leaning on the doorway with a bloody lip.

"Time to let her go."

Karl Baker.

My dad.

Forlorn.

A mess.

But here.

And mine.

My arm goes down. And the blame falls through my feet.

Wherever she is.

Wherever she flew away to.

She can take it with her.

"You are so strong, Marcie."

A smile.

Then the tree miaows. High up in its black branches.

The unmistakable squeaky miaow of a cage-fighting kitten.

☆

You in the camping chair, your dad on the step, me on the floor.

All three of us staring up at the dark tree.

Everything is glowing.

The fire is fading.

It's done.

What happens now?

"How long are we supposed to wait?" you say.

Your dad scratches his head. "As long as it takes, I guess."

He starts to roll a cigarette. "Instinct will kick in at some point. She must be hungry. Survival first."

Calvin miaows from the tree just to prove she's not dead. I think of the cat on the bin. A mind can't exist in two worlds.

You roll your shoulders and point. "Can I have one of those?"

Your dad smiles, handing you his finished roll-up and starting another.

I think of Leyland.

Checking out.

Choosing to.

The real us lives in dark corners.

You hold your cigarette to the fire and then take a drag to make it burn.

You look older.

You are older.

Something touches the back of my neck, but, when I turn round, there's nothing there.

"Maybe we should call Dr Dolittle Morgan?" your dad says, pointing up into the tree. "He probably knows some ancient cat call from Wakanda or something."

You both laugh. I laugh too, but no sound comes out.

"You owe him one hell of an apology," you say, throwing your half-finished cigarette on to the fire. "He had a concussion."

Your dad nods. "What can I do?"

You sip your drink. "I think he's writing something. He'd probably die of joy if you took a look at it."

I look at my paws. Watch them flicker.

"If he liked my book, Mars, he's probably got terrible taste, right?"

"I wouldn't know, Dad. I haven't read it."

"Oh." He cracks a smile. "I always figured you just thought it was shit."

He laughs to himself. "Full of surprises, my girl."

He watches you, like he's seeing who you are and someone else as well. Someone you have in you.

A quick rustling sound, the scratching of claws on bark and a frightened miaow as Calvin drops on to the cobbles of the alleyway like a dark apple.

She shakes her legs, sneezes, then trots into the yard, past my feet and jumps into your dad's lap.

"Hello, trouble," he says, cuddling her to his chest. "Had enough adventure for one night?"

He stands up, holding her close. I look at her. She looks at me.

And smiles.

"I'll give her some food. Douse this before you go to bed, OK?"

You nod. He leans down and kisses your head with so much tenderness, I have to look away.

"Don't forget these," you say.

He takes his pages. "Thank you, special girl." And he goes.

You stare into the fire. The flames have settled into a slow waltz, and I can feel myself slipping. I have one last thing to do.

"Marcie."

"Want to watch *Harvey?*" you say. "Like we used to?"

I smile.

"Perfect."

☆

Elwood P. Dowd says goodnight to the security guard as the metal gates close.

We're lying together on the shop sofa, under my blanket, you behind me, chest against my back, breathing together in our miniature midnight cinema. The black-and-white picture flickers from my laptop screen on the table.

Something stops Elwood from leaving. He leans back towards the bars of the gate and they open again.

"I love this bit."

"I know."

Elwood smiles up at his imaginary friend.

"Why, thank you, Harvey. I prefer you too."

They walk away together as the strings build and the white words appear.

THE END

"Best ending ever."

I pull your arm around me and squeeze it as the screen goes black. Slithers of street light sneak through the gaps at the edges of the shop blinds. The dark heaps of thrown books look like rubble.

"I prefer you too, Thor Baker."

I close my eyes and I can feel your heart beat against my back.

The *lub dub* of aortic and pulmonary valves. The science of feeling.

"Are you OK?" you say.

"I'm not sure. I feel . . . kind of blank."

"Blank is good. Ready to be filled."

Close my eyes. "Yeah."

I feel your mouth next to my ear. "I need you to do something for me."

And I see you. On the floor. Legs crossed. Ten years ago. Here to save me. Just like I needed.

"You're leaving, aren't you?"

Your breathing stops.

"Yeah."

☆

"I don't want to," you say.

I'm fighting to breathe as you stroke the back of my paw.

The weight of your head on my arm. You are seven. You are ten.

You are thirteen.

I close my eyes. "*You have to.*"

You are nine. You are eleven.

"But I need you, Thor."

You are nearly eighteen. You are twenty-one.

"*Marcie, I am you. Don't you see? I'm the part of you that shows up when it's needed. And that part will be there, inside you, ready to fight when you have to.*"

"But it's not the same."

“No. It’s better. I am wherever you are. Always.”

I am falling.

I am parting from the real.

I lean in.

Your body tenses. You are crying.

“Marcie, please.”

And you know.

You know I’m right. I have helped. And now it’s time to let me go. You have to say the words to make it real.

“I love you, Thor Baker.”

A kiss on my paw.

“And don’t you come back.”

Your voice becomes music as I start to drift.

And then

with a smile

I fade.

What is this?

What do you think it is?

Am I dead?

Do you think you're dead?

I don't know. How did I get here?

How do you think you got here?

I'll punch you, Alan. Stop answering questions with questions.

Would you prefer answers?

I'm serious.

You're not dead, Thor. It's Thursday.

What?

You did it.

I did what?

What you were made to do. The choice. You put her first.

And now I'm here, with you?

Exactly. Now she's ready.

You're not making sense, Alan.

How do you feel?

I don't know. Last thing I remember I was with her. Lying down; she said the words, to let me go, then I don't know. I felt myself float and then . . . nothing.

Nothing?

Not nothing nothing. Just nothing around me. Air. And black. And I was moving. Like I was flying. It felt like I was flying.

That's good.

What is this, Alan? How am I here? How are you here? What about the fade? A mind can't exist in two worlds. I should be gone.

You are.

So where are we?

We're here. **Where we've always been.**

Stop doing that! Just talk normal, please. Where are we, Alan?

In her.

Who? Marcie?

Yes. It's all her.

What is?

All of it. In her mind.

All of what?

Everything.

I don't understand.

Yes you do.

But how?

Quite incredible, isn't it? What the human brain can build when it wants to.

It's all her?

Every last bit.

That's not possible.

Isn't it?

What about the others? Blue? Leyland? Everyone else.

All of them.

And you?

Me too. Impressive, right?

The castles? The train? Fridge City?

All her.

Everything? This desk? That crappy plant? Your bubbly fart water?

It's a lot to take in.

I don't . . . But . . . What about this? Us, here, now?

This too.

Holy shit.

Quite a mind, right?

It's unbelievable. It's unreal.

Real is but what we make it, Thor.

And we're still here?

We are.

But I can't go back?

I'm afraid not. Your purpose has been served.

So what do I do now?

What would you like to do?

Can I still see her? Can I still watch?

Of course. You can do whatever you want to here, Thor. Anything is possible in her mind.

Yeah?

Yes.

Whatever I want?

Whatever you want. You helped, and now you get to see who she becomes. All you have to do is close your eyes.

And will she know, Alan? Will she feel that I'm watching?

What do you think?

Something scratching. Metal on metal.

You open your eyes.

It's early enough to still be dark.

You're in the cot bed in the back room.

Dad is crouched down by the old filing cabinet. He's wearing his jacket.

"Dad?"

"Hey. Sorry. Didn't mean to wake you. I was going to leave a note."

There's a click and the bottom drawer cracks open.

"You have a key? Where are you going?"

"Oxford," he says, standing up, "Diane's folks' place."

You sit up, rubbing your eyes. Your hair is flat on one side.

"Diane? Does she know you're coming?"

He shakes his head. "I think it'll work better if she doesn't. She's special, Mars. I just need to let her know."

"What will you say to her?"

He sits down at the desk. "Haven't thought that far yet."

"What's in the drawer?" you say.

He looks at it. "The real us lives in dark corners."

"Dad?"

"That's what she used to say, your mum. It was like her mantra for process. The real us lives in dark corners, Karl. If you're not willing to go there, you shouldn't even start."

He looks at you. "No more secrets, Mars."

Calvin scampers in from the hall.

Your dad scoops her up and stands. His shirt is buttoned up wonky.

"I thought, maybe, you could stay here, with us? This could be your room?"

His smile is nervous.

"Is that what the clearing-out was for?" you say.

He nods. "If she'll come back, Diane will be in with me."

You picture it. The three of you. The four of you. And it feels right.

It has felt right since the first night you slept here.

This is where you should be.

"I'd like that, Dad."

Your dad actually appears to grow, like he just caught a power-up.

"I've left money on the table upstairs for food," he says. "I'm taking this one with me." He strokes Calvin's head. "What's a last-ditch quest of the heart without a feline sidekick?" He nuzzles her head with his nose.

"We might be back later if it doesn't go well. I'll call you. You'll be OK for a couple of days if she lets me in, right?"

"Yeah. Course."

"Morgan can help with the shop. Tell him I'd love to read anything he has, you know, if it's useful."

He goes to leave.

"Dad, wait."

You stand up and fix his buttons. Calvin purrs.

You smile. All around you, a backdrop of Fridge City.

"Tell her no more Alton Towers."

Dad nods.

"Thank you."

And he leaves.

You click on the lamp and squat down at the filing cabinet. You slide open the bottom drawer and see piles of old typed pages, bulging journals and files packed with clippings. The smell of old book.

On top of everything there is a Polaroid photograph, washed out by time. A woman with cropped black hair and a narrow face stands in front of an open fire, her body tilted, arms outstretched, as though about to dance.

You stare at her face.

She is looking to the side. At something beyond the camera.

Somewhere else.

You flip the picture over.

There's no date. No scrawled words. No message.

You look at her again. At the piles of Dad's old notes.

A drawer full of the past.

You drop her back in and push it closed.

Taking your sketchbook and pen from the desk, you get back into bed. Sitting up near your pillow, you open the book and look at your sketches. The buildings. The details. The characters. Me.

There is blank space. Waiting. You touch it. Feeling the possibilities, you grip your pen.

I see you, Marcie.

Do you feel me watching?

You look up.

Out.

Right at me.

"I feel you, Thor Baker."

Then you smile.

And start to draw.

☆

There is a door.

A simple panel bedroom door. It's open.

Stepping out, a boy with bear arms finds that there is no floor. Only sky, all around. And he is not scared. He's smiling as he reaches out for a girl. She's smaller, wearing a dark hoodie that's way too big. Her fringe is cut straight above her eyes, and she's smiling too.

At the boy with bear arms.

Helping him to fly.

Oath of the Made

Born of purpose, formed to be

Parts of self, longed to see

Some to work, some to play

None shall speak, of where we stay

Let us listen, make us feel

Or send us off, from all the real

We give ourselves, until the fade

We live for you, we are the made.

ACKNOWLEDGEMENTS

Thank you for reading my book.

Writing can be lonely. Roaming through your own head with a notebook or at a laptop, trying to figure out what you are asking yourself and the universe, it's easy to get lost in the woods. Luckily, I have amazing people close to me who get as excited about talking characters over breakfast and bath-time as I do, and help me find my way through every story I try to tell.

I call them my family.

They're ace. Thank you. x

Yael, for being the person I trust with those most important things, ideas. I love you.

Sol, for the gift of Blue and your incredible comics. I love you too.

Dylan, for our big conversations about time and the universe that help me work out what I think. I love you too too.

Thank you,

Cathryn, for being Cathryn. I'm lucky to have you. Lily, for your skills. Nick, for your patience. Sam, for all your work with the details.

Jenny, for the walks.

Thank you, Barbara, for reading so much when we were seventeen that I started reading again to try and impress you.

And finally, thank you, Megan.

In a world full of bad news and angry headlines, vacuous posts and poisonous fluff, your email arrived at such a perfect time and gave me just the boost I needed to make this story the best it could be.

I am truly grateful.

Steven